Dedicated to

"MERLIN" TRAN

William P Thomson

ETHEREAL

AUSTIN MACAULEY PUBLISHERS™
LONDON · CAMBRIDGE · NEW YORK · SHARJAH

Copyright © **William P Thomson 2021**

The right of **William P Thomson** to be identified as author of this work has been asserted by the author in accordance with section 77 and 78 of the Copyright, Designs and Patents Act 1988.

All rights reserved. No part of this publication may be reproduced, stored in a retrieval system, or transmitted in any form or by any means, electronic, mechanical, photocopying, recording, or otherwise, without the prior permission of the publishers.

Any person who commits any unauthorised act in relation to this publication may be liable to criminal prosecution and civil claims for damages.

This is a work of fiction. Names, characters, businesses, places, events, locales, and incidents are either the products of the author's imagination or used in a fictitious manner. Any resemblance to actual persons, living or dead, or actual events is purely coincidental.

A CIP catalogue record for this title is available from the British Library.

ISBN 9781528918909 (Paperback)
ISBN 9781398432390 (ePub-e-book)

www.austinmacauley.com

First Published 2021
Austin Macauley Publishers Ltd
1 Canada Square
Canary Wharf
London
E14 5AA

Table of Contents

Ethereal 1	7
Quoras	32
'Amourae'	57
Ethereal 2	74
Yurei	107
'Alone'	129

Two years had passed since the storm phenomena had swept across the globe and a calm had settled upon the land and in the minds of humankind.

Ethereal 1

A New, Human Reality

The Telling of an Unseen Madness

Door open, small group into an average looking room, of adequate size, present and preserved. An ordinary receptacle in which the extraordinary was to be made known.

The group had already been primed to the small matter of a segment of the Official Secrets Act, and one that had not been activated in years: **The Traitor's Act**. If found guilty under its terms, the person or persons would be shot to death by firing squad, within an hour of sentencing: within the Tower of London.

The group assembled consisted of the Heads of the main Departments that collectively made up the British Intelligence Service and parts thereof. Hereinafter, referred to and written as BIS, for the sake of brevity and convenience. There were three women in the group, one of whom being the British Prime Minister.

There was a group of chairs in front of a dais at one end of the room to the singular door entrance, itself manned by a Military Policeman, hereinafter simply referred to as the MP. It was he who had guided the members of the group to their individually designated chairs. The Prime Minister's was front and centre, with the Director General (DG) of BIS seated to her immediate right.

And then there was the dais itself. On it, to the left as you faced it, a lectern, upon which a large, closed, black covered folder. Next to it, what could not be observed directly by the seated group, was a pen and what appeared to be a television remote control unit, which it was, after a sort.

Behind the lectern, to the right as one viewed it, a sixty-inch screen television. Not a conventional one for the consumer market, but one for BIS alone, so constructed and programmed to accommodate specific needs, one of which included an in-built video CD facility.

The overall mood of those assembled for the Briefing, for that was the expressed purpose for them being there, was somewhat sombre yet expectant. After all, this was a most extraordinary meeting. Were a bomb to fall upon it, the British Intelligence Service would no longer exist, save in title alone. There had never been a meeting like this one, nor any remotely like it. It was a league beyond even COBRA.

Enter The JINN

And then she entered the room. A tall woman, fine of feature and figure. Conservatively dressed, and seemingly deceptive in age than her overall appearance suggested. Businesslike in her manner. What struck one most on first seeing her were the eyes. Large, almost unblinking. Clear. Light, icy grey in colour. Like steel orbs. Whatever else, obviously not a woman to be trifled with. The soubriquet it seems someone in BIS had bestowed upon her being 'the JINN'. Somehow it seemed to suit her, both as regards to her manner, her knowledge and achievements within BIS. It was said that when she heard of her uncalled for soubriquet, she was not altogether displeased. That aside, she was not into tittle-tattle, unless it served the Service in an immediate, operational way. Some did say it proved she had a little feminine DNA strand, thus proving she was human, and a female, if not necessarily that humane. Of course, by comparison, men of a certain age and standing were full of it! As to humour, it was there, in a rather intangible, sometimes caustic, sarcastic way.

And why 'the JINN', most often simply abbreviated to 'JINN' for convenience, at the expense of grammatical correctness?

A JINN is a creature in Jewish mythology, and originating from Arabian mythology, and said to perform all sorts of acts of magic and enchantments. Of one thing there was absolute certainty to those who knew of the woman (real name jealously guarded) and came under her influence, usually indirectly: that she had total command of her craft. That's to say, the ways and means of the dark arts, complete knowledge and experience of the world of espionage. The very few high enough, and superficially closest to her, called her 'BRITANNIA'. A lady, and the epitome of all that was British. Of her voice, her speech, what to say? At best, in personal situ, as soft and sweet as honey; in matters of business, diluted vinegar. In full on, Defence of the Realm mode, vinegar in extremis, laced liberally with acid.

The small group watched on as the lady arrived at and stood before the lectern. She gave the hint of a smile and nod of acknowledgement to the Prime Minister. As to the others present, it was as though they were not present, at least as individuals. The JINN opened the folder as she looked over to the MP at the door, giving an imperious motion with her hand as she did so. The MP took his leave, closing the door after him. The small group heard the metallic sounds as the door went into 'lock safe' status.

It was time. Time to speak of a madness unseen.

The JINN spoke, her voice being clear, without emotion. She might just as well have been addressing a group of students. A little distant, very matter-of-fact.

JINN:

'My name is of no importance. To those who may know of such things, it seems some refer to me as a JINN. Even '*THE* JINN', accrediting me as the definitive. You picks your grammar, you takes your choice'.

There was just the slightest indication of surprise from a few of those present. Was that her almost legendary style of humour they heard?

It did not matter, the moment had passed. One might have noted that there was no hint of response from either the Prime Minister or the DG. All that followed was strictly business; and some business it was! She continued.

JINN:

'I begin by making it clear to you this is a briefing, and will be, through necessity, all but one-sided. A week from now, after I have spoken to you all individually, we will meet again, and there your collective input concerning this problem will be most gratefully accepted and, I'm sure, prove invaluable. As far as this briefing goes, any questioning must be limited, and then put by just two; our Prime Minister, of course, and the DG himself. I request that any such questions put be brief, concise, limited. Time is not a luxury at our disposal. When we next meet, by which time you will all have more details to hand, and have grasped, to some greater degree, the nature of the problem, you will hopefully furnish me with some constructive suggestions for managing it, if not removing it entirely.

And now it begins, by way of certain words. I ask you to concentrate on that over-sized screen and what you are about to see upon it in the course of this Briefing. I suggest you clear your minds of the other matters of business of your days and put your mindset into that which you employ in your daily duties, not to mention back in your own personal agent days in the field. You, Prime Minister, in your own way, of course. To all present, whatever way you choose, whatever you read and see upon the screen, read and inwardly digest; most especially the words corporeal, ethereal and real: the more so the last of the three. Let that be your anchor, your foothold to retaining your sanity as things progress'.

As the JINN gave the instruction, she had also made use of the remote control to switch on the most uncommon television. The screen lit up in an instant, though nothing to view in the moment. And then they were there, the three words she had especially brought to the attention of the group. These she then proceeded to explain.

JINN:

'Imagine an electrically powered car. The car complete, along with the batteries, represent the Corporeal. The energy created through the batteries, and the power that allows the car itself to function, represents the Ethereal.'

As the JINN explained, she again operated the remote control, and on to the screen, under each of the three words, came written definitions. She spoke them. Clearly, precisely, sans any drama. As teacher to pupils still.

JINN:

'Corporeal. Literally the body physical; material as opposed to spiritual. Ethereal. Literally airy, unearthly, delicacy of substance. Heavenly, celestial.'

Again, JINN spoke without drama, histrionics. However, her audience were now sitting up straight, paying rapt attention to the great screen, with the occasional glance to the speaker, who herself went on. Some sensed just the hint of a picking up of speed as regards to her delivery.

JINN:

'And now the third word, and quite probably your saving grace: REAL. Definition being that of actually appearing. *Actually existing as a thing, occurring in fact. Genuine.* And, for you, the anchor to hold fast your sanity.'

The JINN had placed far greater emphasis in the explaining of the last word. Again, by use of the screen, she froze the image of the words, whilst also pushing some other buttons. Nothing seemed to happen. It would, in time. All things come to those who wait, but who would probably neither understand nor appreciate the coming.

The JINN seemed to pause for just a moment, gather her thoughts, and then onward went.

JINN:

'I am now going to introduce you to one of our few special interrogation units. Two rooms, side by side. Not interconnecting, each having its own door for entrance and exit. Even so, there is a connecting item. Essentially, a two-way mirror of some considerable size. From the interrogation room position, it is just that; a mirror. However, from the observation room side, it's a window. The whole thing is fitted with an audio-visual recording system. Hence, we have a film record of every interrogation. Of course, some of you here know that. We move on.'

The JINN pressed a button on her remote control and the screen sprang to life once more. Gone the words. Now the group beheld the interrogation room. The JINN pressed her remote control 'HOLD' button and the picture "froze". Onwards the lady went.

JINN:

'You're now observing the interrogation room from the observation room side. Soon you will see numbers down in the bottom right hand corner of the screen. These give days, dates and times. And now a statement of fact and an apology. We have edited what you're to see simply for sake of time. Also, what you *do* see is in real time and real. I repeat: REAL.'

The JINN allowed a moment of pause, in order for what she'd said to sink in, then went on.

'The man you're about to see is an MI7 agent, who we simply refer to as JB. Some of his colleagues enjoy calling him 'Joe Bloggs'. In truth, his real name is Joseph Blogges, as in B-L-O-G-G-E-S.'

Some form of acknowledgement to the humour of the name might have been expected. None was forthcoming. Forever onward continued the JINN.

JINN:

'In appearance, one might use the term that he looks 'well fit'. As to who he is, where he came from and so on, I will explain more when we next meet. All by word of mouth, not committed to paper: for anyone.

So, your patience is now to be rewarded. You will see this film twice, because it was filmed twice. There is no trick photography, nor computer generated imagery. God, I wish there had been. All is not the real reason why you're here, but the problem that *now* faces us. First, the first film of the, shall we say, 'happening', as I'm sure it is simpler to express it so.'

The JINN pressed another button and once more the screen was "live". She turned herself fully to face the screen.

What followed the first time had to be seen to be believed. What followed the second time was because no one could believe what they witnessed the first time, and they hadn't seen the half of it.

The setting, 'stage' if you will, of the interrogation room was a little odd in itself. There was an ordinary metal framed single bedstead in the centre, opposite the singular door to the room. Upon the bed, a bog standard, rather worn and not well holstered mattress. Placed up against the bottom rim of the 'mirror', a table, upon which a large student note pad. On top of that, a black ink biro, complete with cap. Interesting to note, an absence of chairs. The stage was set.

Madness Unseen

The JINN pressed the PLAY button on her remote control and the 'show' began, with her making occasional comment

The door into the interrogation room opened inwards, a man stepped into the room and closed the door behind him, not taking his eyes off the bed before him.

JINN:

'This is agent JB. Six feet, two, well set, as said. Note his hands. Somewhat wide, thick, muscular. Fingers likewise, but in proportion'.

JB moved with an ease. Relatively good looking, dark of feature. He appeared calm, focused, wearing a light blue cotton, short-sleeved shirt, outside of his dark blue jeans and was bare-footed. He moved to the bed and laid upon it, face up, arms at his side.

In moments he'd closed his eyes and seemed in sweet repose. It was like a silent movie, albeit in colour and the sound on and functioning, as was made apparent when the agent took his place upon the bed. Without notes, and eyes firmly on the screen, the JINN pressed the PAUSE button as she spoke.

JINN:

'It was from here we edited, simply to spare you the boredom of much inactivity. The agent had asked for one complete week to demonstrate, or not as might have been, what very particular skill he had. He'd asked for the first minute of a Monday, on through to the last minute of the following Sunday. In fact, it took him just over three days. What you will now see, or not in some respect, began at three minutes after midday on the Wednesday.'

The JINN pressed PLAY, and once more action followed. One minute nothing, then a sound of the mattress being pressed down on the side nearest the observation window. Some seconds passed, then next all witnessed the biro on top of the student note pad on the desk being lifted, the cap removed, the pad opened and then the biro writing, seemingly of its own accord, several lines. This done, the cap placed back on the biro and the biro laid by the side of the pad. Needless to say, the onlookers were agog, making muted utterances, each to his or her own self. At this moment, the JINN once more pressed PAUSE.

JINN:

'Please observe closely the edge of the mattress closest to the window'.

She then pressed PLAY and the *unseen* action followed. In a few moments, the group witnessed once more a depression in the edge of the mattress closest to the window; as though someone, some *thing* had sat then laid upon it. And that was it. The JINN pressed the PAUSE button, turned and once more addressed herself to the group.

JINN:

'The agent awoke, if that's the right term, minutes later. He seemed to take a little longer to become fully awake and aware. When he eventually reviewed the film, along with others, myself included, he was as surprised and as disappointed as we as to what had been there to see.'

DG (Asking with barely suppressed anger):

'Which was what, exactly, ma'am?'

JINN (Giving calm reply):

'That which you shall see in just a moment. Also, I remind you of those three words I addressed myself to earlier, and for your collective benefit.'

The group's attention was now firmly on the lady, but collectively, displayed excellent, professional discipline. Even the JINN was impressed, so gave them encouragement by way of compliment to their manner.

JINN:

'Over the days that followed, in discussion with a few of our senior scientists and medical people, with input from JB himself, a course of action was determined. In brief, they put a special red tinted filter over a second camera and filmed the content of the first camera's recording. What you will *now* view is that filmed by the second camera.'

As the JINN had pointed to the sixty-inch monster behind her, she once more pressed the PLAY button, as all turned their attention to the screen; trepidation being their companion viewer of the moment.

It was indeed a re-run of the first viewing, albeit this time seen through an extremely faint tinge of red.

It's what else they viewed that was of a truly fearsome hue. It seemed that some apparition was rising upward from within the body of the agent. As it rose above JB's body, it swung its legs over to its left side of the mattress, then seemed to glide with effortless, ethereal grace to the table. It was of size and proportion to the agent, but devoid of human feature or bodily detail. It did as the astonished onlookers had viewed before. The taking up of the biro, then writing into the student pad and return of the then capped biro. He then returned to the bed, depressing of the mattress as it moved onto and in the same positioning to its host body, and from there, absorbing itself into the selfsame, host body. At that point, the JINN made use of the PAUSE button, followed by the OFF button. No immediate comments ensued. How could any follow *that*! The JINN could, had to, and did.

JINN:

'In terms of space, one of my advisor's had likened what was happening as not being dissimilar to what might happen within Event Horizon. In brief, making redundant the laws of physics totally. As the days after progressed, we leant more than that which the scientists had declared: contradictions. There was substance to JB's ethereal state, as witnessed in the fact that it could hold objects, the pen, and depress a mattress. It could bump into things. It, Blogges' Ethereal Self could, seemingly, float through the air, but not pass through solid objects. One also learnt, in a minor way only, thank God, that if his Ethereal Self were to hit something, or be in some way wounded, the bruise, cut and blood would appear on his Corporeal Self. Such facts as these tended to limit his 'super power' status, one could say.'

DG (seemingly becoming interested):

'Can he breathe? Does he, *It* have a heartbeat?'

The silence following the question was palpable. JINN calmly gave answer.

JINN:

'JB's Ethereal Self neither breathes nor bleeds, whereas his Corporeal Self does both, as said. When the former is outside the latter, the former's heartbeat is one every ten seconds. It can be lower; once in every sixty. And for the record, when his Ethereal Self is separate from his Corporeal Self, the latter cannot be seen reflected in any mirror.

The film you have just seen, both versions, was made more than eighteen months ago. JB can now do separation within an hour. He also informs us, in his ethereal form, his senses are greatly heightened, his physical strength, if I can even put it that way, also considerably enhanced. He believes his thinking and attitude becomes different, acute. As he himself so succinctly explained: no superman he.'

From the DG another question, and somewhat lighter in context as to what had preceded it.

DG:

'What did it write in that student pad?'

The JINN's answer was matter-of-fact, as if it were a simple matter under discussion.

JINN:

'In the student pad, something of some substance. A sort of paraphrasing of the Hughes Mearns poem come ghost story: 'Yesterday, upon the stair, I met a man who wasn't there. He wasn't there again today. I wish, for I, he wasn't there at all'. Also his distinctive copperplate style of handwriting was as usual, with his letters slanting to the left, and still writing left-handed.'

A bemused silence, followed by a typically, of the moment question from a member of MI6.

MI6:

'Are we just sitting and observing this phenomena, ma'am, or actively dealing with it?'

JINN:

'Well, if it's of any comfort, our higher and betters within BIS have allocated a pronoun to any who are able to separate in this way: 'Separates'. Such a practical contribution, I thought: not!'

Muted laughter and appreciation of the put-down was expressed.

And then came harsh, practical considerations from the Prime Minister.

PM:

'Where does all this leave us? What can he do? What can we allow him to do? What, if any, control do we have over him? Can a human being do such, such separation?'

The questions had been calmly put. Also, she had not addressed the JINN by her sobriquet, nor in any other way. For the first time, as the JINN addressed herself directly to the PM alone, whilst actually answering, she gave a passable smile.

Even so, she only answered, as regard to the last of the questions.

JINN:

'I appreciate the practical content of your questions, Prime Minister. However, until our next gathering, I give answer only to the last of your questions.'

The JINN then proceeded to do so, and the answer she gave did not best appease the concerned recipients.

JINN:

'Yes, agent JB can do separation, but only as you have witnessed; from his Self, producing also his other Self: his Ethereal Self, so they co-exist at one and the same time. However, in another context, he is not alone. In literature we had 'Jekyll and Hyde'. Actors can become other 'selves' any number of times.

Tragic though it may be, there is the mental condition referred to as 'multiple personality disorder'. As an agnostic, I feel free to state that the oldest, most famous 'separation' Man is told of, and millions believe, literally in good faith, is that of The Three in One: Father, Son and Holy Ghost'.

There were murmurs of disapproval. The JINN gave a none too gentle slap of the lectern as she responded.

JINN:

'With all due respect and deference, we are not here to debate philosophy or matters religious. However, *I* am here to talk of one known to us all, unfortunately: Tregora. The freelance 'Butcher of Europe'. I'm glad to inform you that he is dead. I'm loathe to use the word assassinated, as that is a term reserved for those of genuine political standing, but a category to which he himself was deluded enough to believe he belonged. A 'crusading, avenging' one at that, as he called aloud to the nations many times over.'

Assassination Unseen

At this moment, and somewhat against type, the JINN paused, almost possibly hesitating as she viewed those before her. She then appeared to take a deep breath before proceeding to tell of an assassination unseen.

JINN:

'What follows is, what our American friends might say, an extreme bottom-line explanation as to the demise of Tregora. When we meet next week I shall, hopefully, offer a little more detail. Be it so, what you hear now will be sickening enough in content.

In this presentation, I must declare the raw material is courtesy of eye-witness accounts and the subsequent postmortem reports on Tregora, and all of which were translated, assessed and put into a sort of narrative form by my personal staff, which include some excellently qualified men and women of Medicine.

On a given day, at a given time, at a given location, JB, in his Ethereal form, gained entry into the late Tregora's private residence. The butcher had his usual coterie of guards, thugs and butchers all, together with his three closest, named by Intelligence as Vlad, Drac and Hannibal. These three, with Tregora, were secreted within the butcher's most private of rooms. All, save Tregora, were carrying arms, as were many of the guards in a large ante-room.

At the killing time, Tregora was in full rant, claiming he was the God of Europe, and soon to be of the world, which would fall and tremble at his feet. A little ironic, as the psychotic moron barely made five feet four in his bare feet. A Napoleon complex, blended with a liberal dose of Vlad the Impaler, Hitler and Stalin, to name but a few infamous butchers past. I suppose you could throw in Pohl Pot for good measure.'

All who listened, who knew of her, had never heard her speak in such a way before. Was it possible she was justifying the action taken against Tregora, and the secrecy of same in its literal butchery as to the manner of his removal from life?

The lady continued on, now well into pace and delivery of her tale of retribution.

'JB had no trouble getting up and into the considerably large ante-room, then simply waited for Tregora to scream out for something or other. When the door into the maniac's inner sanctum opened, JB simply slipped in, being careful not to bump into any corporeal bodies in so doing.

Once Tregora's immediate needs had been attended to, the minions departed and the door closed, JB attacked the target head-on. At this point, you have to remember, neither Tregora nor his three faithful guards could see a fifth person in the room. Once the attack commenced, the three could not understand what was happening. Of one thing their collective moronic mind could fathom was that the attacker was directly in front of their leader, so they simply couldn't fire their weapons directly at him. Suffice to say, they were firing left and right and above Tregora, for all the good that did. They gasped, screamed, cowered even as they fired away. When the others burst into the room, they immediately thought Vlad, Drac and Hannibal were shooting their leader, so fired salvos at them. Two died within minutes, the third, Hannibal, survived long enough to croak out his version of the madness. And who but the mad would believe such madness?

Even so, the one who had cradled the dying man, heard enough to repeat the man's dying testament. Others ended up shooting at each other. It only ended when they beheld an invisible force hurtling their dead leader some twenty five to thirty feet into the back wall of the room. On impact, Tregora's mutilated head disintegrated like an exploding pomegranate, blood, brain and gore flying out in all directions. The remains of the man had fallen to the floor like an eviscerated, discarded rag doll.'

Silence, looks of disgust and revulsion on the faces of some, save the Prime Minister, who was expressionless. Shock can get you that way. Brief pause concluded, the JINN continued.

'JB's Ethereal Self had used just its hands, accompanied by, what my medical people agreed, had to be uncommon, unnatural force. He had put his open left hand behind the man's head, whilst placing his open right hand, with fingers spread apart, across the face. He placed thumb and index fingers to one side of the man's nose, middle and ring finger to the other side of the man's nose respectively, squeezing as he did so, cutting off that route for breath to travel. The palm of his hand was over the mouth, so cutting off the air supply from that route. He put the heel of his hand under the man's chin. And, with such positioning of his exceptionally large, muscular hands and fingers, began the horrific process of squeezing the life from the man, whilst at the same time, pushing his hands forward, thus creating a vice-like action. In short, JB's other Self was both suffocating Tregora and crushing his skull at one and the same time.

Thus the following, sickening fragmentation of Tregora's skull. The cracking, splintering, coming apart and, eventually shattering of the component bones that make up the human skull:

Ethmoid, Frontal, Occipital, Pariental, Sphenoid and Temporal. We must not forget the eight so classified 'auxiliary' bones of the cranium: Zygomatic (the cheek bones); the Maxillary (which forms part of the top part of the jaw); the Nasal bone (that forms the bridge of the nose); the Vomer (that divides nasal cavity); the Palatine (that forms the roof of the mouth).

I list these, as best I can, and courtesy of both the details from the postmortem report, and the interpretation of same by my Medical people, simply because ALL the aforementioned bones were so decimated as I have described. I have been assured that JD was *not* instructed as to the manner in which he was to kill Tregora. He merely used his own knowledge and skill to end the ghastly man's existence.

From the witness testaments, it seems Tregora first stopped his ranting suddenly, his eyes expressing extreme fear and bewilderment, as he began to gasp for air. His face seemed to flatten somewhat as his nose suddenly spurted copious amounts of blood. His eyes then seemed to be drowning in blood, and the sounds of cracking, splitting bone could be heard. His left eye suddenly shot out of its socket like a rounded pellet, then left dangling on his then somewhat misshapen left cheek, simply by dent of the attendant optical nerve. They saw the man's teeth cracking, then shooting out from the mouth like miniature bullets, then falling to the floor. His gums had split open horizontally, like the earth parting during an earthquake.

It was believed that by this time, Tregora's black soul was already on its Hell-bound journey. His bodily waste and fluids were most certainly leaving his body! Prior to his deceased, wretched body being hurled backwards towards the far wall, his head was a bloody, misshapen mess. Only as it hit the back wall, did the head, or what was left of it, "explode". It's hardly surprising only one of his guards had noted that at his last, Tregora's body was some inches off the ground, as though his limp body had been hung out to dry, prior to its brief journey to the back wall of the room.'

JINN ceased her narration. All within the room were somewhat stunned. It was possible that the Prime Minister even shed a silent tear, perhaps believing no human being should suffer such a death, even Tregora.

After the brief pause, the JINN gave her reason for so graphically describing the death.

JINN:

'The reason I have recounted the death of Tregora in such graphic detail is because I have set in motion the creation of a special department within BIS, which will bear the title Department E. This by way of indicating that its business will be all matters concerning that which is completely new: and so termed by others as Ethereals. Not only to us, but to the world at large, albeit they probably don't know about it: yet. At present, my people are putting together two sets of profiles on Agent JB; before and after. His mental and physical person as a complete human being, and when in his Ethereal state. It seems that in the latter, he has the physical power and strength of a gorilla. Of the mental state, that of a homicidal maniac? A Tregora in all but name? Yourself notwithstanding, Prime Minister, I will be counting on each of you contributing to the compiling of these profiles; most certainly the latter. In essence, and to paraphrase, we need 'to know our enemy'.

It would be a few years before two others would put all the pieces of information together, like a jigsaw, and so produce a picture of an Ethereal and what *It* actually was.

DG:

'And where is our 'Separate' or 'Ethereal' now? Be he, they, enemies or friends?'

The DG's questions had been cold and harsh, the JINN's response measured, sans emotions.

JINN:

'He is now designated as agent 0013, and has recently enjoyed a brief CryoSlumber, and is presently going through psycho evaluation. After Tregora, it seems he still has some residue of physical and mental fatigue.'

Once more the DG to the fore, with a somewhat barbed observation, disguised as a question.

DG (Repeating a phrase heard earlier in the Briefing):

'So long after the assignment? No superhuman he, then'.

The JINN did not rise to the bait, simply deciding her audience had been briefed enough, so began a closure, beginning by closing the folder in front of her and switching off the giant TV.

Closure

JINN:

'Sufficient unto the day, good people. Door!!'

All jerked in their seats as the JINN had called out instruction to the MP, who was outside the closed door. It opened in an instant, as all arose from their seats and turned to depart. As they did so, the JINN had stepped away from the lectern, stood down from the dais and made her way to the Prime Minister, guiding her away from the others, to have a quiet word with her. The exchanges seemed amicable enough, the JINN showing just enough grace to acknowledge the Prime Minister's position and power in the hierarchy of power.

The exchange of views and comments concluded, the JINN escorted the Prime Minister to the door and to the care of her personal bodyguard. With all departed, the JINN slowly began to make her way back to the dias. She pondered on the meeting. Not bad, all things considered. The second would, hopefully, be more constructive; positive approaches, profiles completed, profiles made. One could but hope.

As she reached the dias, the JINN looked up to the lectern. A moment of hesitation, of recall. The noting that the folder was open, being sure she had closed it. She had.

For what reason she was not sure, she felt an edge of fear in her thinking as she stepped on to the dias and approached the now open folder.

As she looked down to the title page of the document therein, her blood froze, her scalp tingled as she read the scrawled words, and seemingly written with her own pen.

What had been penned was easy enough to read, the handwriting all too familiar. Copperplate letters, slanted slightly to the left. *His* handwriting. As she read, her blood ran cold: **'Shall I then also be as Cain to my own Abel?'**

Had he been there, in the room, heard and seen all? Was he still there? Here, there, everywhere, or not at all anywhere, now? Or never, ever there?

With her renowned mind, power of will, the JINN entered into a wholly different mindset. Time to confront a specter of the Ethereal kind. And she believed she knew where.

With a measured stride and speed, the JINN departed the room and made her way to a small lift secreted in a corner of the corridor and proceeded to descend into the bowels of the MOD building. From there, she made her way to the two-roomed Interrogation unit, now acting as a temporary medical room to serve the needs of agent 0013. Once there, she saw that the sole door into the Interrogation Room itself was open.

She stood at the entrance for just a moment, first looking to the bed in the centre, to the attending physician and the nurse, then to the mirror on the wall to the left; therein the reflection of the individual upon the bed: JB, in the whole. His Ethereal Self inside his Corporeal Self, as proved by the reflection displayed.

As she stepped into the room, the Doctor looked up, seemingly somewhat surprised that the JINN was there. How did she know? Who had told her, if at all?

The JINN moved over to the bed, totally ignoring those present. She looked intently down at the body before her. Face ashen grey, slight, bluish bruises to left and right sides of the nose. A like bruising around the mouth. Both eyes and lips partially closed. Death by suffocation, and gently done. The Corporeal Blogges appeared quite dead, and at the hands of his own Ethereal Self?

JINN:

'How did he get in, Doctor, knowing as we do he, *It*, cannot pass through solids?'

DOCTOR:

'We check …. checked on the Corporeal Self on the hour, every hour. The room being rather warm, we left the door open. After all, the nurse and I have been the only ones in attendance today.'

The JINN nodded her head in acceptance of the explanation given.

JINN:

'And the death?'

The man of practical, everyday Medicine was at a loss to explain. He did try.

DOCTOR:

'Suicide, ma'am?'

The JINN gave the strangest of smiles and came to the Doctor's rescue.

JINN:

'Voluntary self-euthanasia of his Corporeal Self at the hands of his own Ethereal Self, Doctor. You left the door open. It entered and did the deed, and gently so, as best as one can observe from the bruising and relative calm look of the face. But who will ever really know? Don't worry, I'll provide as to the ways and means to those few who should know. No others.'

A somewhat relieved Doctor proffered forth his own overall summation.

DOCTOR:

'Odd really, ma'am. It began here and it's ended here.'

The JINN turned to the Doctor, staring hard at him, then seemed to soften her gaze a little. The nurse had left the room.

JINN:

'Wrong, Doctor. It began years ago, somewhere in Japan, we believe. I take it you know why it's ended this way?'

The Doctor did not answer, so the JINN obliged.

JINN:

'It, Blogges as his Ethereal Self, a Separate, entered, did the deed as gently as it could and, in the seconds of his own life left, passed back into his then dying, Corporeal Self. Probably holding his breath at the very last. The whole complete once more; and dead. Problem eliminated. For the real Blogges, enough was truly enough. But then, who really knows, Doctor? Who truly knows?'

A somewhat weak explanation given, and her plaintive questioning thereafter confirming the madness of it all, the JINN made her departure, giving final comment as she did so.

JINN:

'Here it ended, Doctor. But what about out there? **Out there!**?'

In an ending, a new beginning

Not only had Joseph Blogges passed over, but another was also to follow. Not literally, yet, but to a pasture new.

The JINN had decided enough was enough; of the old way, and her part within it. Others also thought much the same thing. It was time for a new way, a new structure, a fresh life for an old dog; British Intelligence.

She had the way, had drawn up a blueprint, shown it to a few very influential people. They had agreed. The JINN, quietly and unbeknownst to most, was going into retirement, and had been given the parting "gift" of a large grace and favour flat in the renowned British Intelligence Library, for the remainder of her life. From there, with the help of a chosen few, she would instigate her final service to the cause: the creation of 'The Agency'. A truly new, modern British Secret

Service, with a 'Board of top drawer, truly experienced in all the many and varied black arts of their trade, and of the highest academic level, 'Executives'. Also, as need required and demanded, absolutely ruthless in service and defence of the realm.

CLOSE

Quoras

(Hubris knows well its prey)

The old order was gone, including the 'JINN', seemingly. British Intelligence had a new name, 'The Agency', split into Divisions, each specialising in the prime aspects of the "Great Game", as someone past had described the so-called art of spies and spying. Each Division having its own Head, with one all seeing, knowing and controlling Division – and Head: 'The Executives'. For the rest, it was business as usual.

A day of reckoning was at hand. No one would witness it, or hear it. A consequence would follow, but not be realised. The old adage of things not changing, remaining the same, would again be proved true. The bait had been placed, the trap set, the prey seen and taken, only the proof of the conclusion witnessed by one unknowing.

Somewhere, on a drab, rainy day in London, one gentleman called upon another. One of Government, the other of Intelligence. Yet again, ne'er the twain meeting in common accord.

1

Once at the inconspicuous building, the Intelligence gentleman entered. Inside, things were somewhat different. Security was the byword, a certain faded grandeur also evident. The gentleman presented his ID, not that his personage was unknown: Smith. His name was John Smith. His real name known to but a handful; and suspended some years past for Queen, country, security, and his own physical wellbeing. He was servant to his masters, who were 'The Executives' (tE) of The Agency, and well acquainted with matters Ethereal, not to mention the BG. The Watcher of the hour (security guard in the old parlance), pushed a button on the reception desk. No sound was heard. Not in the reception area, that is. Elsewhere, the ring sounded most clearly and sharply, in the office of the Division Head: Quoras; so christened by the Executives of The Agency. He heard and answered. As to his *real* name, no one seemed to know. Seemingly, he had never had one, until The Agency (via 'tE') had 'Christened' him. It wasn't long before some clever senior bugger in the hierarchy suggested he simply be addressed, only by fellow seniors it has to be understood, as Vardis. 'tE' had given him his official name after he had become the Head of UK Amourae, sometime before. On hearing his 'official' name was 'Quoras', the aforementioned 'silly bugger' had suggested that if one laid the accent on the first syllable, the greater emphasis on the first letter, 'Q', it rhymed with Vardis, as in 'Quo Vardis'. It was perfect to the man, as he often asked the question, 'Wither goest thou?' of many a foreign agent; or traitor. For the record, 'Quoras' was Latin, meaning one without soul. In this case, to know a person, in The Agency, check the meaning of their name first.

Sometimes it held the key to their character. In truth, Quoras preferred 'Vardis', knowing as he did, the full meaning and reasoning behind his officially given Agency name.

What interested many, tE themselves included, was that he'd titled his latest enterprise by that very name, ; as in 'The Quoras Project', let alone what the enterprise actually was, and why they were not being kept informed.

And that was why John Smith was there; to find out the reason, and to enquire about the man's health. Also, why the Executives were lacking even the basic details concerning the enterprise. Mind you, Smith wondered just why he'd been given the assignment, and on the 'no questions asked' basis. After all, they had to know their man. Something seemed not to be quite right in the State of Denmark.

A second Watcher came into view, pointing towards a lift, whilst making it clear he was to escort Mister Smith to Quoras. The former declined, making it clear he would himself make his way, knowing exactly where Quoras resided. He had trod this way before. Two floors up, at the end of a small corridor; the door exactly opposite to the lift.

No one was inclined or of rank enough to challenge the decision. And so, a man cold of heart, proceeded to make his own way, to one bereft of soul.

As Smith made his leisurely way to his meeting, he thought upon the one he was about to see; not for the first time. He had dealings before, from time to time; brief but courteous. The only thing that stood out about the man was his voice. Deep, quite resonant, but not as powerful as it might have been. Perhaps his average height did not allow for larger, fuller lungs. Mind you, there was a coldness, an emotional detachment to the voice. It seemed to be making it clear in sound, if not in word, that he did not wish any meeting to linger unduly. Such satisfied John Smith well.

Tick tock, tick tock, tick …….

As he made his way, Smith was changing both his rhythm of actions and his mindset. He was also ruminating as to the circumstances of his 'assignment'. Essentially to find out how Quoras looked, to enquire as to the man's health, what he was about and why he was being so secretive.

Smith had now successfully negotiated the first flight of stairs and was on to the second. Another thing concerned him. The Executives knew most things, especially concerning their own, "new" Agency and personnel, so why all this? 'Direct assessment by one of major position upon another, old boy', was the reason afforded to Smith. Same old story; boxes within boxes, necessary self-feeding of the paranoia upon itself: The Agency. Some things never changed, no matter how "new". More specifically, the Executives Division that ran it and was responsible for it.

Onwards and upwards on to the second set of stairs. Silence, for the better part, would be the heart and way of it, Smith had decided. Once he'd put his questions, concisely and straight to the point, to *look* and *listen* being the *means* by which to assess. Smith had been well chosen for the task. He'd proved down the years that he was par excellence when it came to extracting information, without recourse to violence; verbal or otherwise. He was, after all, a lead Interrogator, and relatively young for the position. Also classed as a 'Civilian'. One other thing, to maintain a degree of civility, Smith would address Quoras as 'Vardis'. Why not, what's in a name? The more so as this was The Agency! New, civilized and 'with it'.

The second set of stairs negotiated, Smith looked ahead, spying the door that led into the kingdom of the soulless being. John Smith was ready. Mindset in place, his own rhythm set, mental 'distance' established. He would not challenge, cross verbal swords. By his own words, look and manner, Quoras(aka 'Vardis') would be judged.

Smith was now outside the plain, but solid looking oak door. He gave a powerful rap on it, making it clear he was there, ready and determined. A pause, then from within, a dictatorial voice giving permission for entrance.

Tick tock. tick tock. tick …

Game on.

2

Smith entered, in a calm, measured manner. As he did so, he deliberately looked to the walls and ceiling of the room, not towards his 'quarry'. Once in, he turned around to close the door slowly, quietly, whilst continuing to peruse the state of the décor. Even before he turned to face the reason for his being there, came the voice.

VARDIS:

'I trust this meeting will be brief, as other matters demand my time.'

The man's voice was, as usual, deep, powerful, sans emotions; cold and distant. For his part, Smith had turned to face the Head of the 'Dark Angels'. And what of this man? Just the same. No change. A total absence of even the basic interpersonal skills. It was as if, in the eye and mind of Quoras, Smith did not exist before this meeting. Also, for the record, whilst The Agency had given Quoras his singular name, by others, in his own little realm, he was addressed simply as Vardis, as he wished it to be. A strange man indeed.

Also, not widely known or spoken of as such, he actually created the 'Dark Angels' concept, and it had proved most successful.

Smith had not stretched himself to judge Quoras in the past, but now had to, in order to fulfil his reason for being there; namely to perform a profile. So now it was a judgment of the moment, as he beheld the man. Briefly, he was a little below average height, hard of look, somewhat battered by his years and his own history within the Intelligence Service, over the years. Such included all but ten years working with the double-0 agents; strictly on the administrative side of things. No Bond he.

Ultimately, as Smith knew, the eyes have it, and the eyes of Vardis provided proof of the lie in his voice. His eyes reflected one haunted by his own history, memories, of failure, within his own mind, and not so far from harsh truth. Whilst the memories lived, the eyes seemed to be fighting to remain so. And the power behind the will were of those memories. Yet, for all this, the man's energy seemed to belittle his look, even though it itself seemed forced, unnatural. A mix of anger and frustration, perhaps?

Because he couldn't have the remarkable Nobel for his own exclusive, personal use? Just Smith's take on the man who stood before him. Even so, it was his assessments, views, and in this case, profiling skills that the Agency paid him for.

As he moved forwards, the man under scrutiny made to preoccupy himself with papers on his desk, itself a grand old and battered remnant of the age past. More to the point, the man we'll continue to address as Vardis, had placed a chair some six feet in front and away from the desk.

That more than suited Smith, and to make this plain to the man, decided to spike his potential adversary's gun, simply by standing behind the chair, realising his visit would almost surely be a short one. At least both men would be singing from the same hymn sheet, if not to in the same key.

VARDIS (Looking up to Smith, whilst still handling some papers):

'So, who are you, why you here? Their lackey, I assume?'

Tick tock, tick tock, tick ……

Looking directly at the man with an analytical, heartless coldness, and answering in a like manner, and being somewhat amused that the man was feigning that he had no memory of meetings past, he got straight to it.

SMITH:

'No, sir. I'm one of the senior Interrogators for the Agency.'

Whatever misdemeanors Vardis had or had not committed in the eyes of the Agency, he was the Head of a Division, which made him Smith's senior in rank. Even so, Smith had wondered why the man hadn't been invited to join the Executives Division itself.

Vardis had now stood upright and erect, looking directly at the man before him, wondering why The Agency had sent, as he saw it, a nondescript. He wondered also what the man before him thought of The Agency itself; if he even had the guts and will to have an opinion.

VARDIS:

'Do you think The Agency is schizophrenic, Junior person?'

Tick tock, tick …

Smith let the implied insult pass him by, believing it to be with a capital 'J', therefore at least a title; after a fashion. As to the man's question, the Interrogator wasn't there to socialise, merely to question. Such being so, he kept his mouth shut.

VARDIS:

'My, my. Dumb, as well as stupid. Typical Agency fodder these days. Then let me enlighten you'.

Vardis sat down behind his desk, eyes still firmly on Smith. One thing was for certain; it would not be a compatible meeting of minds; remembering one being soulless, the other heartless when in business mode.

Vardis sat back in his much used chair, something resembling a smirk upon his face, as though he were enjoying some secret known to himself alone. Who knows, perhaps he was about to sing his swan song.

As to Smith, he'd seen such displays of egotistical bluff and arrogance many times over. Different reasons, locations and personnel. Still, every dog deserved its day. Trouble was, who *was* the dog this day; Vardis or Executives?

A surprise move from Vardis. He swung his chair to his left, so then facing away from Smith. Why? Dramatic effect, embarrassment, or the signs of resignation, surrender? None, if one were to judge solely on voice.

VARDIS:

'Have you never questioned the names; 'Agency' in the singular, or 'The Executives' in the plural? The former implies a singular body in charge, whilst the latter, a number of people in charge'.

There followed what writers might term a 'pregnant pause' then Vardis continued. Whilst his voice conveyed a degree of interest, it was as cold and distant as ever.

VARDIS:

'Do you know how many Executives there are? I'll tell you. It varies. At the moment it's ten; that's A to J. That leaves sixteen to go. Seventeen if you want to be pedantic about it. All based on the alphabet. As to reasons, it's said that it spreads responsibility and also prevents any one person controlling all'.

At this juncture, even Smith was interested, although he did not betray the fact. Was Vardis just pissing in the gravy, or was there a truth in his words? Indeed, was The Agency a sort of modern day Inquisition, with TEN Torquemadas? Smith allowed himself a brief smile, but in mind only, as his look betrayed nothing.

Suddenly, Vardis swung back around in his chair, once more facing Smith directly. Back on with the circus, with the former being the ringmaster of the moment.

VARDIS:

'So, what do your masters want of me? What are you here to spy?'

The game was now on, thought Smith, ball now firmly in his court. Mind you, Vardis, or Quoras, remembering his true Agency non-de-plume, had one more surprise to deliver; shortly.

SMITH:

'They want to know about your health, why you haven't volunteered exactly what you're in the process of putting together, and why you've given it, whatever *it* is, your own Agency given name, and why you seem to be taking so long.'

VARDIS:

'That's it?'

SMITH:

'Yes.'

Vardis got up from his chair, stroking his chin as he did so, staring hard and steady at his Interrogator. Then, as he gave answer, came also that other surprise.

He pulled out a small bright red box, which could fit into an average sized pocket. He opened it up, took out an elongated, torpedo shaped, bright red capsule, returning the closed box back into the right pocket of his jacket. He then spoke.

VARDIS:

'What's the time, lackey?'

As he'd barked his question, Smith was suddenly aware there was not a single clock to be seen, neither on wall nor desk. He couldn't quite see if Vardis was wearing a watch. He gave answer as he glanced at his own watch.

SMITH:

'Fourteen minutes to midday, sir.'

Smith was a little surprised in his formal addressing of the falsely named Vardis. Even the latter's look seemed to soften for just a moment. He then poured some water from a small crystal decanter on his desk, into a whisky glass close to the decanter and proceeded to swallow the capsule, with the help of a large gulp of the water. Whilst replacing the glass on the table, he spoke once more.

VARDIS:

'Close enough. Right, as to your impertinent questions, I give answers. It took me three years to think through the 'Dark Angels' concept, the third year in testing it out. I'll reveal *MY*

Quoras Project when I'm ready. As to the name, my concept, my prerogative, and all good things take time. Now if you're done, you can go forth and multiply back to your masters!'

Smith believed he'd identified the singular reason for the state and attitude of the man: he'd gone "rogue", driven by ego as much as anything. Bad combo.

Smith was spared deciding what immediate course of action he should take, as whilst hurling the coarse, yet intellectually acceptably delivered command of dismissal, Quoras, by true agency name, had pressed an unseen button under the rim of the desk on his side.

In rapid response, two Watchers had entered the room. That was it. Game over. Smith gave a wry smile, thanked Quoras, turned and made his way out, flanked by the Watchers.

As luck would have it, a taxi was passing the building as he walked through reception and out of the front door. He hailed it down, deciding the mode of transport gave him time to think before reporting back to his 'masters'.

As Smith exited the room, Quoras called out questions, yet almost as an insult, an accusation.

QUORAS:

'And what of the JINN? Where is she now? Did we kill her, or perhaps even *them*; the Ethereals!?'

Smith kept going, not looking back, disregarding the jibes. Even so, in his mind the echo was there.

Such were his thoughts and musings as the cab whisked him away from the madness, which he thought was the general state in Quoras land. Seriously, as the man hadn't acknowledged the Executives as being his ultimate bosses, as they were Smith's. Therefore, Quoras was, in effect, acting outside of The Agency, as an entity and law unto himself. Not good, not good at all. If such remained the same, something bad was sure to follow: retribution. But, for whom, when and how?

Tick tock, tick tock … STOP.

3

As Smith mused his way through the brief journey, he allowed his body and mind to relax, his inner clock to stop, his en garde mentality to go back into its box until required once more. In another mindset, Smith prepared himself for what he would report back to the Executives. Putting his thoughts together, in a sequence; all in order and to an order. An order out of chaos (of another's mind and ambitions). Smith allowed himself a wry smile; this time clearly on his face, and not restricted within his mind alone.

As the taxi drew closer to a small building, but a stone's throw away from one of the more illustrious Agency abodes, Smith requested it to pull up. He'd decided to stop for a quick coffee at his favourite little coffee shop, then walk the last part to his appointment with the Executives. And so it was. Once refreshed, he concluded his brief journey on foot.

As he approached the rather small and drab looking building, somewhat to his surprise, four Watchers came out of the main entrance, walking purposely towards him. When they reached him, one turned in front of him, so leading the way, the second and third took their places to the left and right sides of Smith, with the fourth of the Watcher quartet getting into step behind Smith. The whole brief pantomime was more amusing to Smith than sinister. He knew immediately he was being escorted directly to the Executives. He did ask the question, to no Watcher in particular, as to the reason for his unrequested escort. One obliged with an answer, with just a hint of amusement.

WATCHER:

'Cause the Executives were a little concerned about your whereabouts, Mister Smith, not to mention just a little peeved when they spied you'd taken time out for a coffee'.

The Watcher had provided the answer in a simple, straightforward manner, accompanied by a knowing smile. Smith gave a slight bow of acknowledgement and thanks to the man, also reciprocating the smile to the subtle humour.

Would the Executives be so relaxed and obliging to him when he gave details of his visit to Quoras, Smith wondered.

Then they were there, swallowed whole into the place of spooks, deceits, deviousness, betrayals and treacheries; and that was just amongst the occupants themselves. Shortly, another could be attributed to the whole: murder.

In what follows, there will be a marked absence of detail of place and personnel. In and of themselves, not necessary, as the narrative will be all.

Smith, with just the single Watcher escorting him once in the building, journeyed in a lift into the rarified atmosphere of the higher realm of The Agency and to a meeting with one of the Executives' foremost leaders.

4

By any other name

The lift came to a halt, the single door sliding silently open, the escorting Watcher then leading Smith out straight into a room. Having delivered him, the sole Watcher took his leave. It was a case of a different 'game on'.

As to the room itself, somewhat disappointing. Although quite large, it was bereft of any sort of fixtures and fittings one might have expected, the walls quite bare. Hardly Executives standard. Drabness personified. Civil Service, boned down to the core. Even so, all was not without interest. There were three items of furniture. Quite a large table and two chairs, one behind it as one faced it, the other in front of it. Mind you, there were things upon the table; papers, some folders and a box.

However, it must be said, he that sat behind the table was every inch a person of interest. City dressed, yet fit in both look and physique. His eyes positively radiated authority, the face full of bonhomie, quite relaxed. Still, John Smith had seen such before, on the faces of certain others within the senior ranks of The Agency. Such being so, he knew the man could, in an instant, deliver fire and brimstone in both verbal and physical manner. Although, something about the face; a private worry perhaps?

It didn't worry him, as he knew of this man, and his reputation. The Brigadier General no less. One of the top good guys; one of the very best.

BRIGADIER GENERAL (BG):

'Pull up a problem and sit yourself, John Smith.'

As the man had spoken, he'd given a reassuring smile as he pointed to the chair on the other side of the table. His voice was strong, modulated, and only a slight vowel and consonant off being pure Oxbridge.

John Smith approached the vacant chair in a firm, measured stride, as he viewed the man before him. He was of the belief he could be in for a different sort of game; chess, after a fashion: Agency fashion!

BRIGADIER GENERAL:

' I hope you enjoyed your coffee, young man'.

The man had leant forward as he made the comment, smiling as he did so, but with his eyes firmly on Smith. He then relaxed back, giving a short, genuine laugh, as he gave a last riposte.

BG (From this point onwards):

'Cheeky bugger, but good for you. Now to business.'

As the BG finished, Smith gave a smile of relief, but also noting, immediately, the man's change of tone. Hard, direct, with just enough hint of friendliness; as one on the same side as the other; only with more power and gravitas at his command.

SMITH (answering as in response to a direct order):

'Yes, sir'.

And so the de-briefing began, surprises and all.

BG:

'Briefly, Smith, a profile of the man you know as Quoras, if you please'.

The following verbal manner of Smith's profile of the said Quoras quite surprised the BG also.

It was almost automaton in nature, and delivered in almost exactly two minutes. Only on two occasions did the man behind the table express any sort of acknowledgement, and only then by a glance. The word "rogue" and mention of a bright red capsule

After Smith had spoken his take on the man Quoras, there was a moment or so of silence.

The recipient of the information given, leant back with a smile of satisfaction, not to mention relief on his face. Excellent, young man. Precise, without conjecture or subjective opinions. For his part, Smith had thought it best he should mention the accusations the man had made, so added the codicil. The BG listened impassively, then gave answer, without any emotion one way or the other.

BG:

'Our', 'The Agency' by name, is fit and well, living in a degree of comfort and safety, which is no more than she deserves. Sticks and stones are of no consequence.

As to Quoras, thank God for that, John Smith. Had it been otherwise, it would have been a removal without good cause, albeit that it had been as civilized as possible.'

Smith expressed some signs of puzzlement at the BG's comment. The latter gave explanation.

BG:

'Quoras is dead, Smith. His body was found within minutes of your departure. At first, they thought you were the man's murderer; indeed still view you with a deep suspicion. Hence, our Watcher guard as you approached this building. Reprisals can be sudden and final'.

The BG had attempted a comforting smile, but it was not entirely successful, as was clear from the look of concern on Smith's face. Then the BG took over the de-briefing totally, as he took the box on the table and placed it in front of himself, proceeding to speak as he did so. His voice was, clear, firm and friendly. Also, full of the authority invested within him.

BG:

'Right, listen and observe, John Smith, and don't interrupt.'

The man's last words in the instruction were abundantly clear, but accompanied by a genuinely warm smile, this time much appreciated by Smith, as he leaned back, relaxing a little and paying the greatest attention.

BG: (opening the box and removing two smaller boxes from it; one bright red, the other dark blue, tapping the red one as he spoke about each).

'I take it that you saw a red box like this one on Quoras' desk?'

Smith nodded in the affirmative.

BG:

'But not this one, I assume?,' questioned the BG further, wishing to be sure as he tapped the dark blue box.

Again, Smith nodded, this time in the negative.

The BG sighed in acknowledgement and launched fully into explanation.

BG:

'Quoras had a particular heart problem; Tachycardia.

Simply put, his heartbeat was faster than it should have been, but not too much so. Mind you, if he got excited, it would become more of a problem, very occasionally triggering a brief faint. Well, a few months ago, our Pharmaceutical people produced two very special capsules; one bright red, the other dark blue. For the sake of simplicity, we call the former 'red lightning', the latter, 'blue slumber'. The 'lightning' increases the heart rate, whilst 'slumber' decreases the heart rate. In time, we'll make an adaptation of these two medications available to the NHS. However, *these* also have within them what can be loosely termed as liquid tracers. In short, any who take either one also becomes traceable. Not only do we know the state of the individual's heart at any given time, but where they are geographically. The tracer element can last up to a year; unless they up and die, in which case, game over. Trace stops.'

Even speaking in a low key, matter-of-fact manner, the implications were not lost on John Smith. The BG spoke on, whilst opening the red box and removing a bright red capsule to show Smith, then returning it into the box, replacing the lid and then both boxes into the larger box.

After which he then sat back in his seat and continued seamlessly to continue his narrative, sans pause for breath.

BG:

'And now, returning to you, John Smith. Not only are you an outstanding interviewer, as well as an interrogator, but also, by default, profiler. We have known about Quoras' activities and general demeanor for some time. From a distance, you understand. Even so, it wasn't enough. We had to have an up close assessment.

For this, we had our own man, a certain Major, get in closer, keep us informed. He seemed to confirm the situation. For all that, we had to be absolutely sure, as what we had in mind would be a permanent solution. Hence, we sent you, a professional, experienced profiler, to assess the man. We simply could not activate an 'extreme prejudice' act, be it by any other name. We had to be certain. After all, he is … was … one of our own. You have provided that certainty. Even so, the best laid plans of mice and men …'

The BG trailed off for a moment, then went on, in an upbeat tone and mood.

BG:

'Our people buggered things up somewhat. They had the 'red lightning' delivered to Quoras a day early. At ten PM.

Hence, he took the first of the four-times-a-day dosage at eight AM the following day, TODAY; the day you went over to see him. So, when he took his second capsule, which you witnessed, just before midday, there was no way back. For the record, the dosage was set at eight AM, midday, four and eight PM. We wanted to be sure! Our Pathologists will pronounce that Quoras died of a massive Myocardial Infarction. That death was almost instantaneous. His particular heart condition, allied to the stresses and strains of his work and position will be attributed as the primary causes. Of course, it would have been better if you had not been there, but we couldn't have everything, I suppose.' The offending items, the red capsules, were removed by one of our "cleaners", so termed.'

The parting shot was delivered with a certain grim humour, with smile to match.

Smith was taking it all in, but not without some difficulty. He had to ask the obvious question, so did so, as politely as he knew how.

SMITH:

'What had the man done, sir. How so terrible as to warrant his mur ..... .'

An uncharacteristic silence from the BG followed, then answer given.

BG:

'That's a good, humane question, John Smith, which deserves an answer. 'Murder', so said by his people. You will not be aware of them, let alone seen them, but we have two very special lists within The Agency; one red, one blue. The red one is, in crude terms, a 'kill' list. Those people verified as traitors and foreign agents acting against our Nation and allies. The one in blue are People of Interest, and Quoras was on it, until yesterday.

We're not absolutely sure about them. Until we have proof positive that they are foreign agents or British born traitors, they stay on that list. If the proof against them becomes absolute, then they're moved on to the red list and, as and when, the act of extreme prejudice against them is instigated. Call the act by any other name you care to employ.

There is another absolute. No such action can be taken until and if they're moved on to the kill list. There's no debate in this regard. We know as fact, that Quoras ordered the killings of two on the red list, along with a further two on the blue list; two women!

We also believe he was running his own small, private 'Murder Incorporated' business; arranging killings for personal gain.'

The BG had spoken in a hard, unyielding voice, and John Smith had listened in stunned silence. One would have needed a chainsaw to cut the atmosphere.

The BG then continued, in hard, unrelenting manner.

BG:

'When we, the 'Executives' were absolutely sure, we set about verifying the mental state of Quoras. In this, we made use of an observation by the late Nobel's own words in his 'Testament' and, finally, you Smith. By happenstance, it was at this time, our Pharmaceuticals Division came up with the capsules: in particular, for our purpose, the red ones. Once a few have been taken by one with the Tachycardia condition, their heartbeat goes through the roof, resulting in heart-attack and death. Our Pharm wizards are working on a liquid version of the capsules. Easier to administer. Isn't science wonderful!?'

The BG had concluded with the cynical, rhetorical question, his voice cold and flat, as he stared at a somewhat subdued, "lost" Smith.

He continued, in a more straightforward, practical manner.

BG:

'As to the so-called, egotistically named 'Quoras Project', therein, a tragedy wrapped in a cloak of hubris.

Here one can reference a number of great, singular achievers, such as writers and composers, not to mention one-shot 'pop singers'. Each in their turn have one resounding hit, be it in words, music or what passed as 'music and song'. Thereafter, each in their chosen artistic way, strove to repeat their success.

Alack and alas, in all but a few cases, ending only in reprising their one-shot wonders. Such was the case with Quoras, and his superb one and only concept for the Intelligence Services, that did, of course, become The Agency; his own 'Dark Angels'. I'm afraid from time to time, some of our own, including the agents with the double-O prefix to their name, go rogue. Asking other agents to kill them was not really satisfactory or desirable. So, 'outsiders', in a manner of speaking, were brought in.

Their allegiance being to country and Agency alone. The man Nobel was a prime example and, tragically, through him, came the first indications of Quoras himself going rogue.

As to his grand new concept, a non-starter. To take those who had just one skill, so described: to kill. Worse still, to recruit those so-termed 'skilled to kill', no matter from where or what background. The misfits, the dregs of society. Neanderthals with gun, knife or bare hands. The only exception probably being Nobel himself; and probably not entirely 'of this world.' In their defence, it can be justifiably said that many in the field of Intelligence, are employed because of some deviant skills, of one form or another. Ours is a shitty, immoral business much of the time, Smith. Bear that knowledge well.'

The BG had finished, seemingly lost in a reverie of memory. He then energized himself by slapping his hands on the table as he jumped up, quite taking John Smith unawares.

BG:

'That's about it for now, John Smith'.

Smith had stood up, but had a question of his own.

SMITH:

'So, you're closing down 'Dark Angels', sir?'

Suddenly, the BG was all positive energy and bonhomie, as he smiled at the much confused young man before him. Prior to, he'd thought the BG had ignored their past involvement, with the Ethereals. Not so, the BG took each matter in isolation. Nothing personal.

Time to wrap up and conclude.

BG:

'Forgive me, John Smith, where's my memory and manners, eh?. In short, no. Quoras' Project is dead in the water, 'Dark Angels' very much alive.

Someone will be promoted and become Head of the Division. As to you, young man, stay close, I'll be in touch. I'm charged with taking a more personal interest, involvement with this entity called 'ETHEREAL'. I have an excellent lady with the unfortunate name of Slaughter, but the looks and body of Munroe. Better still, she has brains and knows how to collect and assemble information, collate and present an overall picture. Even so, she may need help, and another with such ability may speed up the process. I'll explain if I call on your service and particular skills'.

John Smith took a deep breath as he smiled, his mindset and rhythm already changed into the 'be set, be ready' mode

SMITH:

'Yes, sir, I'm ready, but in truth, I haven't quite taken it all in yet.'

The BG looked in a sympathetic way at Smith, as he slowly moved around the table until he stood full square before the young man, then whilst shaking Smith's hand, spoke soothing, encouraging words.

BG:

'Don't worry, John Smith. If I, we, didn't think you able to the tasks we may ask of you, we wouldn't ask you! But remember what I said; we're shop-soiled, dirty, nasty people, albeit still on the side of the angels: just! You'll be free to decline if we decide to bring you on board. In the meantime, you need to clue up on Ethereals, although none of us truly know what they are, where they're from, how they got here and what they intend. Not that I'm discouraging you at all! You'll get to read most of that bumpff (the BG pointed to some files on the table) and be schooled by specific specialists within the Executives.

And, you lucky man, you may find yourself tutored by the delectable Slaughter. But hands off, like you, she's Government property! Maybe also another of the female gender; we'll see.

The BG then turned and made his way back behind the table, as Smith dared one last question, which both surprised and delighted the BG.

SMITH:

'Sir, how does that 'lightning' capsule work?

The BG laughed and smiled at Smith, seemingly delighted by the young man's somewhat out of the blue question.

BG:

'Bravo, you, Smith. Begin as you mean to go on. Question. Question everything, take nothing for granted. Well, simply, as explained to me, we all have electricity coursing through our bodies, via our cells. They in turn act like start up motors, generating energy into our heart and lungs, not to mention providing the 'power' for our brains. Our little red lightning capsules increases our internal electricity, its power. If you want chapter and verse, read Langham and Burr, Hodgkins and Hunley and Watson and Crick, but in your own time. All things being equal, you'll be otherwise engaged, for me. Right, times up, so up, up and away! Don't bother about clearing your desk, that's been done whilst you've been with me.'

That was it. A surprised, somewhat bamboozled but smiling Smith, accepting his lot. The BG had banged once on the table as he called out a single word: 'WATCHER!'

A Watcher appeared from the lift, which John Smith hadn't even heard ascending, unless both lift and the poor bugger inside it had been waiting to be summoned in due course. Wondrous, indeed, were the ways of The Agency!

Smith followed the Watcher into the lift and down, not once looking back to the remarkable BG and wondering what would come next, or who the bloody hell the Ethereals were!

As he stepped out of the building and into the daylight and fresh air, he thought but one thing as he smiled broadly: **game on!**

Another thought went fleetingly across his mind. Why did the BG seem a little uncomfortable in his seat? Is that what had made him jump up at the closing of the session?

As Smith was both happy and relieved, so too was the BG as he'd won the day against his fellow Executives, telling them it wasn't only good policy to keep possible enemies close, but also identifying and bringing fresh blood and more brains on board, such as Smith and most likely the woman Flowers. BG hadn't actually recruited Slaughter directly himself to the cause, but did agree, as she had the pedigree for the task.

Simply stated, the BG's mindset was indeed resetting itself, preparing to face what he thought quite probably a greater threat: the 'ETHEREAL'. Present, unidentified and with intent not known; save it could possibly not bode well …. for Humankind. The more brains to identify and combat *It/Them* the better. But the BG's greatest enemy was within: his own body.

end

'Amourae'

Testament
No Ordinary, But Extraordinary Life

'Call me Nobel. I was born a bastard. I also grew up to be tall, naturally strong, and with an attitude to complement my birth. I was not one of noble intent. In matters academic, my attitude and demeanor meant I was asked to leave several schools.

I was out of the educational system by sixteen, and spent a few years in and out of work; usually the latter. However, as said, I had physique, standing a solid six-five, well set, physically strong and into gyms. Someone suggested I turn my physicality into some money-making work. I did. I became a bouncer. It wasn't too long before a few jobs came my way. Even so, I was deemed too enthusiastic in my work, and once again found myself out of work. Then, things changed. Someone in one of the gyms I used suggested I learn about physical discipline, perhaps learning via Martial Arts; both the mental and physical aspects of them. I did, both night and day, seven days a week. I also set about improving my education; to a degree, that is. Also to improve my speech, so I ceased to be like a wannabe Brando on Mogadon. Six years later, my physicality and outlook to life and future was all but set. I also learnt a few others things about myself, but as I'd had no part in their existence or development, I won't go into them. *One thing's for sure, they most certainly helped me in my line of work; much to the delight and surprise of many, and of some concern to others, but not a problem for me.

* * * *

One evening, whilst at some social rave up, Nobel suddenly felt somewhat hot and a little confused. He stepped out for some fresh air. He was alone. As he leant against a wall, he fainted, albeit it but for a matter of a few seconds. He remained in the upright position. Had someone gone to him and assisted him, and then moved on, unseen?

Then, within a few minutes, he was fully conscious once more, much refreshed and feeling somewhat different. He couldn't articulate it, but it felt good. He could not know, but something had visited him, and he would never know who, why, or what. He didn't worry, just accepted it. By the night's end it had been erased from his memory. In reality, he had encountered an unseen entity that simply wished to sample an inhabitant within the strange world in which he, It found itself and that one day would enable him entry into The Agency.

He and his kind who, before too long, would be termed as ETHEREALS.

* * * *

I was pointed in the direction of a company that provided professional bodyguards. They gave me a job. It proved interesting. I met all sorts, brushed shoulders with celebs, and those who thought they were. It was okay, but a bit too glitzy, false and unreal for me. My mind was set on other things.

By this time, I was well into the Martial Arts, and other, not widely known ways and means. I read a great deal on each, then took to adapting and improvising; as much on the mental as the physical side.

For me, this 'new world' was both exciting and exhilarating, and I had no wish to lessen my efforts to be with it, know it, live by it. Perhaps that's why I felt different, but would never know why, including those abilities physiological I had not known that I possessed.

One day, I received a 'phone call. Some person or persons unknown seemed to be interested in me, which made me curious about them and what it was they *seemed* to be offering me. It appeared my name and abilities were being noticed in certain quarters. Some might put it slightly differently; that I had 'gained a reputation'. I wouldn't know about that. I did know they had my 'phone number and address, and that I hadn't given either to them. A day and time was agreed for me to be picked up and taken, 'not so far away', to meet my potential, would-be 'benefactors'. The caller was a man, who spoke posh and with natural upper class authority. Mind you, he did make what I thought an odd request; that I be sure to wear a suit and tie. My first instinct was to invite him to take a hike. I held my peace, saying I would oblige. My curiosity was roused, and what the hell, I was a big boy and could look after myself.

And so the day and hour arrived, as did a gleaming, official looking black limousine. The windows were darkly tinted. I conveyed casual, polite calm. I was not what I appeared to be. Let us simply say I observed the Boy Scouts number one rule: 'Be Prepared'. I was.

From here, there are details I'm personally obliged to leave out. No traitor I. Another will fill in the gaps where he deems necessary and appropriate, keep a flow to the narrative. Let's just put on record that, before my little trip on the day was over, I had incapacitated three so-termed, 'Dark Angel' agents, and almost a fourth. Also, unknown to me, unofficially been recruited into British Intelligence

* * * *

As to what is being revealed from this juncture, much is down to me, although still written in the first person singular as Nobel had started it, and wished it to continue as such when they were his words. Even so, for the record, my name and rank is Evan Tomms, Major. *As to the why and wherefores of my involvement… My main function was screening those brought to the attention of The Agency.

That's how I came to know of the remarkable man named Nobel, and "lost" him in a thrice to the Executives Division of the Agency. Pity really, I had him earmarked for and as a 'Dark Angel', on a permanent basis. Also, in passing, I too had, without knowledge, encountered that unseen entity, and would not have memory of it for a considerable time.

Three years later, I played my part in assisting Nobel in writing his 'Testament'. It was the least I could do for a remarkable man. All I can say is, I did ask the reason for it, but he would not give answer, merely confirming that we shared a certain aspect of disillusion concerning our mutual

'masters'; the 'Executives'. That it would be read by them alone, no others, myself notwithstanding, when the day came. "New" the re-vamped British Intelligence may have been, but power play, internal struggles for a bigger share of the pie, and POWER, continued in much the same old vein.

At the time of my first hearing of the man Nobel, as said, I was involved in the 'recruiting' process. In the case of one such possible, I arranged what some were to eventually refer to as 'the Tournament'. Some three years on, it was he who was to request my involvement in a certain literary matter; to provide, where I believed appropriate and acceptable, details in order to fill in certain gaps , so making a coherent narrative of what he referred to as his 'Testament'.

Ask not for further details on the matter, as it would not serve you well, but I add, to make it clear, that I did not witness the final paragraphs he wrote until the man had passed over.

* * * *

'When Nobel arrived at the secret MI5 location, he was met by a tall, well spoken, urbane gentleman. From there, into a lift, down a few floors, and out into a vast room, that accommodated a full-sized boxing ring at the far end, highlighted by large, well placed spotlights, leaving the rest of the room in darkness. Inside the ropes, four well fit and able looking men, and what Nobel thought to be a referee.

And so, Nobel was instructed to make his way to the ring, enter and to be en garde at all times. He was, shall we say, somewhat pissed off. He loosened his tie, tucking it into his shirt. As he began to walk slowly, he slipped off his slip-on shoes and then, in a human equivalent, went into warp drive. As a writer recorded it, what followed would pass into Agency legend.

In great strides, at remarkable speed, Nobel had suddenly run forward. As he reached the ring, he sprang upwards, grabbed the top rope and proceeded to execute a high forward somersault into the ring, landing firmly on his feet.

Then, the first man had made to attack, in the blinking of an eye, as Nobel landed in front of him, pirouetted, left to right on the spot, then struck out. And so it continued, down the line, felling the first three like trees. It was as a professional laying low amateurs. Even so, his blows had been 'pulled'.

As he'd completed the pirouette, he'd thrust out the outer side of his right foot, straight into the would-be attacker's upper thigh. In an instant, the man's whole leg had become numb, beginning to buckle as it did so. Even as the man himself had begun a slow descent to the canvas, came the second blow. Nobel had thrust out his right arm, right hand up, palm outward. The blow had landed centre to his would-be attacker's forehead. The man had suddenly hurtled backwards into and through the ropes, then crashed downward to the floor. Karate blows, both perfectly executed, had abruptly ended the assailant's participation in the most unexpected private 'tournament'.

Even as the second blow was being delivered, Nobel had seen his second would-be attacker moving in to engage. Another pirouette, as Nobel altered his body stance, until it had been extended to its full height. As he'd done so, he had furled his right hand into a tightly clenched fist, with which he had then delivered as a hammer blow on to the crown of his second assailant's head, resulting in the man having gone down to the canvas as if pole-axed. Another perfectly executed blow. As with the previous man, the blows had been 'pulled'.

Even as this had happened, Nobel had seen the third man coming at him, fists swinging like a bar room brawler, all professional stance, means and method abandoned. It's said that the inactive, supposed referee, had observed that Nobel had displayed a cruel smile as he'd perfectly delivered a second hand blow.

He had thrust his right arm forward, the hand extended forward, fingers fully extended, closely and tightly together, straight into the would-be attacker's throat.

Contact was just below the Adam's apple. As with the previous combatants, blows pulled. No intent to kill.

The hapless would-be assailant had staggered back against the ropes, turned, as if seeking escape from the torments of the ring, before he'd slumped over, unconscious, draped over the top rope like a discarded dish cloth.

As that 'contest' had concluded, Nobel had seen that the fourth man had taken a classic Martial Arts stance; still of body, calm of face. Also, the sign of a slight smile on his lips, in anticipation of the confrontation about to commence. Nobel had, for his part, made the assessment that the man was of the highest order, a true warrior, master of his art: Martial Arts. Perhaps even Ninja trained, if not a Ninja true. Had it been planned as a fight to the death? Is that what those observers in the shadows beyond the ring wished for? And if so, for why? What purpose? No matter, Nobel had seen all before him as if in slow-motion. His actions however had been as fast and potentially lethal as lightning strikes.

Nobel had taken a small step back from his final adversary, whilst still facing him directly, also in classic warrior to warrior stance, giving the slightest bow of his head. His adversary had reciprocated in kind.

At that moment, Nobel had experienced a singular, searing stab of pain in his back, that then, like a fire, had spread across his entire back. He had then felt himself beginning to fall, as if in slow-motion, towards the canvas. Before he'd experienced the completion of his own downfall, darkness had consumed him whole.

The hour and the day had been lost.

All had been in less than two minutes, from the moment Nobel had delivered the first blow upon his first adversary. His guardianship of his own being had failed him; or so it had seemed. In truth, nothing had been as it seemed.

As they had removed Nobel from the ring, a Doctor had, in usual manner, checked for his pulse. To his disbelief, and disappointment, it was absent. To the man of Medicine, fear that someone so promising in the art of killing, was now himself dead.

The Doctor kept his counsel. However, once Nobel was on a stretcher, the Doctor tried again, only this time he included the heart. The shocks continued.

Whilst his seemingly dead patient was sans a pulse of any kind, his heart continued to beat; albeit but twenty to each sixty seconds, and twice over.

By now, others had gathered about the stricken Nobel, totally ignoring the condition of those he himself had felled.

Later in the day, after Nobel's seemingly miraculous recovery, when asked to explain the incredible phenomena of his physiology, gave a direct and honest answer: that he did not know. Then, with something approaching a smug, self-satisfied private grin, noted that he found it most useful if he needed to feign death!

So, it was apparent that, at will, he was able to divide the function of pulse and heart, the one from the other. O, still, my beating heart.

*

Later in the day, in another room high up within the building, the gathering was discussing the events of the morning and, in particular, Nobel's part within it. The meeting was chaired by another urbane gentleman, addressed simply as either 'Sir' or 'Brigadier' by the others, who deferred to him. He himself, as later learnt, had decided that the extraordinary man was for the Agency specifically, and not for any single Division alone. Also in attendance, a senior medical specialist in the field of Physiology; the study of, and understanding of, the implications of the function and mechanisms of living systems; including that of Man.

All were stunned, trying to grasp, make sense of what the specialist had pronounced concerning the man Nobel and his "gifts", if they could have been described as such. That depending if you sided with God or the Devil.

There is little doubt that he was possessed of such, though he himself continued to dismiss them, not understand them, but simply made use of them, as and when. Not knowing how he came by them or why.

His reasoning being that he had not been trained in them, nor worked to develop them. To Nobel, they simply were. No more, no less. No matter, in the three years or so that followed, his physiology and unique skills in the art of disabling and killing were to move his life from the ordinary to the extraordinary.

I was requested to 'keep an eye' on Nobel, as his Watcher, after a fashion, but I hasten to add, not his Controller, thank God!

In spite of what you might think, I was not overjoyed in becoming, by default, Watcher to a freak of nature. Just my view, you understand. Whilst on the matter, I make it clear, I was not the man's friend, nor he mine. Friendships were not encouraged or sanctioned within Amourae, itself the official title for the 'Dark Angels' Division (who I had been intent on recruiting Nobel into), the individual as an Amouree, collectively as Amouraes. As to 'friendships' within the Agency as a whole, as stated, it was not encouraged at all, such being deemed a cancer to the work of the whole, thus cannot be. And yes, three years down the line, my views on Nobel, and also on the remit of both the Amourae, and of the Agency as a whole, had changed, and which resulted in my involvement in Nobel's 'TESTAMENT'.

Whilst Nobel was seconded to the Agency Executives, he was then assigned to different Divisions, often to a man called Quoros in the 'Dark Angels' for "special" assignments, across the whole UK Intelligence spectrum. Whilst such did not please me in particular, having "lost" him as a permanent fixture for that Division, and so incurred the wrath of Quoros, I was relieved that my Watcher role would be at a distance only; and for the Executives alone. And Quoros? That's something for some other time, for others to tell.

And now back to a few salient points from that meeting with the Physiology expert and only those concerning the man's "gifts", as so described by those who appreciate them, or even in awe of them. Most I believe FEARING them. I now simply list, and explain concisely, each in turn; no more, no less.

BRADYCARDIA. When a human heart beats less than sixty times a minute. They did a test on Nobel. He had to run, do press-ups and the like for two minutes, then thread needles; of varying eyelet sizes; from small to very large. He succeeded, with each sized eyelet, each and every time. Even so, as far as his ability to control the ability of both his heart and pulse to order, even separately, was truly history making.

AKINETOPSIA. This is the medical term for someone who suffers a loss of motion perception. The specialist was a little more at home with this. They tested Nobel on his controlled 'ability' within this phenomenon. They showed a film of a cheetah in full running status, with Nobel required to note the distance markers as the magnificent animal blazed its trail. As far as Nobel was concerned, in his truly unique case, it was far more. He could see it at its speed or, in his eyesight, reduced almost to a standstill; on the film, of course.

Those agents he'd laid low might as well have been telegraphing their body stance and positioning prior to every high-speed blow they had attempted to deliver.

Also their facial expressions and eye movements. We were also to learn from the man that, in combat situations, he possessed the ability to hear *his protagonists breathing and heartbeat!*

There were other aspects to these abilities, but not necessary to detail here. However, I think it should be put on record, such skills gifted to Nobel, did not in any way elicit braggadocio from him. Being macho was simply not his way. After all, to him it was a given. As natural as breathing.

At this juncture, I think Nobel himself should conclude the telling of, what is, after all, his own Testament.'

* * * *

'Three years or so, I often did singular assignments for the Amourae Division. And the Killings? No more counting. Reason? No longer certain. Perhaps selective amnesia. That my conscious self no longer accepted, accommodated such statistics; even understood them. Am I perhaps a psychopath or sociopath, or cursed in being both? No, I cannot allow myself such an excuse. Feelings and despair are within me. My questioning?

Two to the fore. Why and for whom? Queen, country, Kingdom; and for the Democratic status within? For Queen, I doubt the good lady had any knowledge of the action, the very existence of Amourae. Certainly not peoples of the Kingdom, for they too share the ignorance of what is done in their name, their protection. However, of those chosen few charged with safeguarding this existence we call Democracy? Yes. They *are* relatively few I think. Those who ply their misguided beliefs, ideologies, egos and status within the blood-drenched cloak of secrecy; in defence of the very thing they claim to safeguard: Democracy, the Realm.

Something more, which I cannot explain. The why, the capabilities within me. As said, they just seemed to have arrived, *entered* me some time past. Why, and from whom, *what!?*

How came I to this pass? This mutton dressed as lamb? This Neanderthal, self-made, honest, false worthy warrior man?

I pause, to give the briefest of explanations regarding my disassociation. Although, as I had understood, I had been recruited with the intent of working for one named Quoras, Head of the so named Division Amourae (known by those within it as the 'Dark Angels') by the person named Major Evan Tomms.

Only then, to be immediately seconded to some unidentified entity within the Agency and commanded by a faceless few, referred to as the 'Executives'. It probably isn't my place to make comment, but what some referred to as the "new" British Intelligence set-up, did seem a bit wobbly at times. "Teething troubles" was what it was passed over as. Even so, it seemed to be that to placate the man Quoras, I was used quite often by Amourae. Names. Such stupid names: stupid, but lethal games. As to the man Quoros, he seemed to be a few slices short of a full loaf. He sometimes seemed to be on the verge of telling me something, then backed off. Weird.

My role within the Agency? Put bluntly, to kill, at their command. Who? God only knew. Enemy agents, perhaps also, those closer to home?

My Controller, at the instruction of his masters, gave me the orders, details and the name of those condemned to die, by my hand; in the true, literal sense.

At different times, and with little reasons as to why, I was charged to take the lives of three WOMEN. Quoros seemed taken by my ways, means and results. As said, a weird man.

To my utter shame, in the early days of my time with Amourae, I did, with energy, zeal and the will to prove myself to my nameless as well as faceless masters, what I believed my duty to Queen and Realm, sans any true inkling of guilt. And remorse? How could I? No sense of wrong to goad or shame me.

The third order to separate a female from her life came in the early part of my third year in the mad, murderous business. By this time my heart, self and soul were no longer in it, my conscience now rebelling. I spared the woman and assisted her to escape to some other country.

I then approached someone who was somewhat of a like mind to my own; somewhat disillusioned. I asked him if he would help me put a few of my thoughts to paper; for later use by those we both served. He did not know the true turn of my mind. In that he was, *is* blameless. Sometime soon after, I embarked on a leisurely walk through the great City of my birth, to continue my search for self and reason. I did not seek to hide and avoid.

One day, someone brushed by me in a small, narrow street, apologising as he did so, then quickly moving on. Later, in what passed for a hotel room, I came across a piece of paper in the left pocket of my trousers. A classic act of 'passing the buck', Agency style.

The note, typed on a laptop most likely, was politely requesting that I, in a way 'Nobel' (sic) to the cause, remove myself from my troubled existence. And yes, I appreciated the capital 'N', so that I would be in no doubt it was me being addressed, by virtue of my name spelt correctly, but out of context with, what I believed, an insincere compliment, as to my act of disobedience and subsequent "disappearance". If I did not comply, would that fourth man, those years past, be sent to confront me? Doubtful. Too old by now I'd thought: or dead.

The reality also being that, as both executioner and victim, I was to serve to my masters, on the proverbial plate, my own head.

A Biblical equivalent, only this being served up to the Devil in human kind. Again, for balance to this 'Testament', those I term in such a derogatory manner, would not, do not see it that way. So, does blind obedience also remove the faculty of human conscience in those bloated by their own ego, status and power driven ambitions?

Mind you, it has to be born in mind that, more often than not, that was how all intended targets were presented to the Agency "executioners", in whatever Division. Fare for the feast, so to speak.

Another, brief walk in a beautiful park within my own country that I had 'betrayed'. One last breath of fresh air as I tried to finally clarify anything more about the Self that now was me?

My illness had gradually crept up on me, become a part of me; a healing that now strives to remove the cancer from my soul, and I from my soul.

This illness, a conscious rampant, entered and now festers within me, by a surfeit of the legalised, murderous madness that is the Agency I have served. Slowly it has been removing my soul, slice by slice, murder by murder. And what does it profit the fool to perform for the Devil?

I tire. Time to die. Forgive me, Evan.'

Unbeknowst to the wretched soul that was Nobel, one unseen was close to hand. *It* could have intervened, but believed such a troubled soul should claim his own rest. Besides which, he had served the need. He had been the way by which to enter into the place where those of other means, ways and power could serve, and where one Major Evan Tomms resided: 'The Agency'.

* * * *

Nobel was found on a park bench in a deserted Kensington Gardens, in London. He was upright, with the first signs of rigor mortis setting in. Eyes wide, unseeing. His jaw was closed tight, his mouth pursed and tight shut. It gave him a strange look of firmness and determination to remain so. No others were anywhere near him. Indeed, there were but a few in the entire park. Some Police, some Military, and all wearing heavy duty face masks.

Once Nobel's body was returned to MI5, an immediate postmortem was carried out, officially instructing as to what it would find. Such would suffice for any who might question. To do so would have been unwise.

All save one, who had scribbled a brief note at the bottom of the last page of a copy of the PM findings, making sure it made its way to a certain Major. This second, unofficial finding, suggested that Nobel had departed the world in a way only he could employ, which also gave reason for the strange look on his lifeless face. He had simply sucked in a last great gulp of air, closed his mouth, then stilled his pulse and heart, refusing to refuel with fresh air. Hence his look of determination (and satisfaction?) at his dying.

To the world at large, officially, it was possible Nobel had joined the thousands upon thousands of good, *blameless souls, who had perished in the wake of yet another Coronavirus pandemic that swept across the globe. Nobel was into his 30th year of life at his passing.*

(Verified by Evan Tomms, Major)

end

Ethereal 2

(The Unseen)

Times *had changed, a new order prevailed in regard to the world of British Intelligence. New name, new structure, new masters. Each area of expertise having its own Division, with a new leader; that's to say, Head. All under the aegis of 'The Executives'. And the architect of all? A retired, rarely seen or heard, elderly lady by the name of the 'JINN'.*

The 'Executives' was a group unto itself, responsible for all Divisions and all personnel therein; 'The Agency', the new, no-nonsense name that covered every aspect of British Intelligence. In reality, although conceived and designed by the JINN, no more a part of her or it. The whole now more corporate in its manner and presentation, reflecting the American input and influence. No more 'cult' personality leaders, unintentional or otherwise. All this not to the liking of all. But such was the way of it, within the always and ever to be dirty, shitty, back-stabbing, loyalty hopping game of spies, and espionage. And, of course, killing. It was ever thus.

Even so, every so often, something, someone, totally untoward and different, would interrupt, in ways that, to put it mildly, proved to be not entirely of this or any other mode of existence. Where the rules of physics simply did not seem to apply. People such as the men Nobel, and Blogges. Then there was the 'ETHEREAL'.

Rumours and counter rumours seemed to rule the days. Then the new order, in the form of the 'Executives' Division, put its collective foot down, with a Brigadier General as was, doing the honours. However, this day he was charged with addressing some senior members from the Divisions, both male and female, along with the British Prime Minister.

As BG took on the brief, and knowing the Prime Minister would attend, he arranged to borrow Colonel Tomms for the day, for the express purpose of receiving the man, and his attending bodyguard, into the MOD, escorting both to their seats and, once the brief was concluded, see both men back to their awaiting car. Tomms' promotion had been somewhat rapid from Major to Colonel. Such was the way of the 'new order'.

For his part, the Colonel seemed happy enough, honoured and glad to make acquaintance once again with the man, BG, who had been a major influence in forwarding his career and promotions. The Briefing took place in an average sized room deep in the bowels of the MOD.

Before the BG, the Prime Minister, his Deputy PM (a woman), the Secretary for Defence (also a woman), a senior member from COBRA, and two 'Executives' from the Agency's 'Executives Division'.

Also present was a Colour Sergeant from SAS Omega (SASO in abbreviation), and several Watchers, doubling as guards on this occasion. The door was closed and automatically locked secure. Two of the Watchers stood impassively in front of it. Another stood ready to operate the main light on the BG's instruction.

As to the BG himself, his Brief was to impart to the assembled, PM to the fore, news both tragic, potentially terrifying in its implications, and most surely the closing of an era. On top of all that, to rally them to face a new, unseen and potentially deadly enemy, it being neither germ nor virus. Not even Man as such.

In this, the BG was more than able to the task, and to be as much the man for the hour as any present. He stood full square and ready, a small table to his left, on which a large hold-all. He called to a Watcher to tone down the lights, which a few moments after were dimmed.

The BG had to hand a 60-inch, "special" TV, along with the necessary remote control. Also close to hand, the hold-all, in the care of the Colour Sergeant from the SASO regiment. Others from the elite, new force, were outside of the room, guarding those within.

A controlled tension was evident, save for one person; the BG. Such a situation as presented, was meat and blood to him. Mind you, he was now in mental action mode: cool, measured, with a certain distance between himself and all present. In mindset, he was close in and personal.

What was to follow was not for the faint hearted to hear. John Smith was in attendance, having also taken up the invitation along with Tomms. Two more able Agency people to hold their own, and BG men, even though Colonel Tomms didn't seem quite his usual self.

It was time. Lights dimmed, the BG turned on the large TV with the remote control, so lighting up the setting somewhat. The occupants of the room were suddenly very still and very attentive. It was 'game on', as the BG was fond of saying.

And so it began. Voice strong, approach direct, the man in charge and command from the off. Although his was a no-nonsense approach, BG also displayed a deft lightness of touch, with his own natural, off-the-cuff moments of humour. His credentials also included both a Victoria Cross and Bar, to go with a Military Cross, also with Bar.

Pressure as such, to him, did not exist. He applied it, was not a recipient of it. Even so …

BG:

'Prime Minister, ladies and gentlemen; I begin. Much has happened of late, leaving a trail of false rumour, in particular almost exclusively concerning the demise of 'The JINN' and the former agent Joseph Blogges. From that also has sprung some anger and confusion.

Hence, I cover that first, and so put it into an order and perspective. In so doing, it is hoped, by the 'Executives', after this you will be better informed, freed from false rumours, and also able to see and move in a more positive direction and mindset from hereon in. You will need to, for terrible and tragic as the details are, there is also, a greater issue before us, and a matter you are acquainted with, to a greater or lesser degree. If I may put it so, matters 'Ethereal'. But be not too fearful. Thanks to the foresight of the late JINN, we are well prepared for what might follow, and also armed in a most formidable way. I have also taken steps to improve our knowledge, but that is for another day. For now, we address the day: *this* day.'

There were some gasps from a few of the gathered, although not from such as the Prime Minister, Smith or Colonel Tomms.

BG moved straight on, as time was of the essence. In himself he remained, calm, unflappable and in complete charge.

BG:

'So, I will begin by making mention of the Library, and then turn to the principals in this drama. Most of you know about the JINN and Blogges as individuals, and the essentials of the sanctioned killing of the man Tregora and what transpired as a result. So, I concern myself with the post-killing event; and in particular the relationship thereafter between the JINN and Joseph Blogges; since classified as the world's first 'Separate', and more widely referred to as an 'Ethereal' I'll deal with basic classifications later. For me it was not unlike the fictional story 'Frankenstein' by Mary Shelley,' as I hope I shall shortly make clear.

First, the Library, inasmuch it is where the JINN resided, in what I would describe as a grace and favour, well-appointed flat, that took up most of the third floor. Also, of course, proving to be the location of her demise.

Many of you know of and why the Library has a capital 'L'. Also, perhaps, some of you should make greater use of it, as it has taken a considerable amount of sweat, tears, blood and guts to put together on the shelves, a record of considerable events, achievements, and failures, not to mention also the storage of cassettes, tapes, discs and film.

All modern communication and recordings of The Agency's history, and of those within; past as well as present. All that you need to know is contained within the Library. By this day's end, you will also be able to visit it, by appointment, to read a copy of this very Briefing you're now attending.

I make reference to the Library on this occasion, simply because it is where, as stated, the JINN met her untimely end. I should also make clear that although the whole surrounding area of the Library, as well as within it, is covered by CCtv;, is sans sound. Also, save in one area: the JINN's flat. CCtv and sound, that is. Perhaps also the saving grace for we viewers, as will shortly become evident.'

The BG then turned momentarily towards the great screen as he held up the remote control to same, pressing a button as he did so. The screen suddenly sprang into life, displaying a "still" picture of the aforementioned building, speaking as he did so.

'This, then, is the Library. I should at this point make it clear I shall, more often than not, confine myself to displaying just stills of those areas I shall be talking about. The JINN was all for giving the film its hour, but that takes up time, even when post-edited. However, we do not have the luxury of such time.

Even so, when I thought it both appropriate and necessary, I had the moving pictures in their place, as I edited. The more so, when the red filter process was employed; not least in proving the existence of the "invisible" Ethereal.

By the way, look to the small building to the right of the screen; it's the left as you come out of the Library. It's the substation that feeds the electricity supply into the Library. Simple brick, with the large, locked steel grate over a reinforced industrial plastic covered steel door. If the electrical supply into the Library fails, there's an automatic, immediate switch-on of the back-up emergency system within the Library. Keep half an eye on that substation. It features dramatically in the last piece of this film.

And now, I deal with the late JINN.'

There was a collective in-take of breath and movement from all present, then silence as stillness resumed.

During what followed, the BG tended to remain facing towards the screen, only occasionally glancing towards his captive audience, if only to make sure they were still awake and attentive. They were, as the BG's voice was powerful and carried well.

'I will give narrative as we progress, and display either moving pictures or stills as we go; all of this re-edited beforehand, at my direction, as already stated. However viewed, it will prove harrowing enough n narrative alone.

Almost three weeks ago now, a Friday. Seven thirty am. A particularly dark and cold morning.

On this day, the recently retired JINN was off to pay visits to both MI Five and Six. Later in the afternoon, she had a private appointment at Buckingham Palace, where she was officially bestowed with the honour of Dame of the British Empire by her Monarch.

Whilst she was away, It, the 'Ethereal' arrived. Also, I switch to moving pictures when I wish you to actually "see" the energy field that is It; the 'Ethereal'.

The BG pressed the remote control once more. Now the screen was more cinema than TV. Also, as and when, the image went into a faint red tinge when the Ethereal was present on the screen, whilst the BG supplied the narrative; just like the JINN in times past.

'If you look to the extreme right of the TV picture, you'll see data figures, one such showing the times. It's now eight-forty am. The morning now a little brighter, though not much. Now look to the left of the film, actually the right of the Library, and you can see it, courtesy of the red filter; that faint red shape is It; the Ethereal. It has come to the Library, to the residence of the intended kill.'

At this juncture, the BG "froze" the picture and faced his audience.

'I should add that over time since the Tregora business, research has been on-going, and of which I am somewhat engaged. Although we don't know if they have genders, I tend to refer to Ethereals as 'It' wherever possible.

It was, again, by the grace and foresight of the late JINN, that the research was stepped up, after the Blogges business. Every aspect of the killing has been dissected via the various postmortem reports and eye-witness statements.

Some of the findings to date make for uncomfortable reading and viewing. For the rest, research and review continues at a pace.

For all that, the best information has come from the comments of the selfsame, late JINN, and those made by Blogges, post the Tregora killing, and during his training time prior to the assignment.

We know It, they, can't pass through solids, can't fly, but do sort of "float" in order to get about. It's also suggested this new species of life is evolving, and further abilities may not be too long in the coming. In fact, correctly stated, it *does* float, or glide; choose your own adjective. This is believed to be due to an electrical field that surrounds Its Ethereal form. Electricity seems to play a crucial part in the life of an Ethereal. In that form, Blogges couldn't see himself, couldn't feel his feet as he moved. He just thought the act and did. He couldn't even feel the force of his physical actions, even when crushing Tregora's skull with his bare hands. For all that, he instinctively knew where his limbs, and appendages thereon, were and when they were in contact with something; human or otherwise. He actually said, at its best, he felt, believed himself to be, a purely spiritual force; and not in any religious context, I hasten to add.

Apart from this, he made it clear that his vastly empowered energy, mental as well as physical, was not of his making, nor his applications of it. It was simply as though he were controlled by some other, external force.

That's as may be, we simply don't know. Make of that what you will. In closing this little collective gem of information, I add a personal, subjective comment of my own.

If these *things* are in any number, and of evil intent towards us, then God help us, as we will find ourselves in direct confrontation with the damned.'

There was a collective movement and audible sound of apprehension and concern. The BG acted appropriately, using his particular style of gung-ho humour.

'Right, good people, on with the magic lantern show!'

He had given his best look of determination and smile, as he looked directly at his Prime Minister, but a few feet from him, front and centre. He knew his own leader, who wasn't called, in some circles, and with some respect, the 'new Winnie' for nothing.

For his part, the PM himself had given a great grin, whilst raising his right fist in gladiatorial manner towards one of his favourite commanders. He knew well enough that he had the right man in the field to lead, should the day arrive.

The BG had turned back to the large screen, his remote control to the ready, the screen image still "frozen".

'Back to It and what follows. Be apprehensive and saddened, but not fearful. We have the measure of these bastards, and the men and weaponry to deal with them; more than you at present know'.

BG pressed a button and the moving images upon the screen sprang into life once more as the presenter continued his narrative.

'We're on film from the CCtv systems now, so allowing us to see Its Ethereal energy field. At this time in the drama, no one knew where Its Corporeal Self, Its own human host body, was located. We learnt later, of course, having located the left-over heap of ashes.

Observe how It *seems* to glide, as opposed to float, towards the steps that lead to the revolving door entrance into the Library. Also note, there is a slight pulsating of the red mass. Our experts are of the opinion that the extreme cold makes this so, as the bastard seems to carry Its own internal central heating system'.

There was a slight, involuntary sound of muted laughter, including from 'Winnie'.

In a moment, all were once more absorbed in the unfolding madness of the hour, silence reigning. The strong, even tones of the BG providing the dramatic accompanying 'music' that was his narrative.

BG:

'As recorded on the screen data, it's now just past eight-forty am. See as it reaches and positively glides up the stairs and pushes Itself slowly through the slowly, *silently* revolving door and into the reception area. No untoward sounds to distract and, of course, nothing to be seen.

I now cut to It as it reaches the top of the stairs at the third floor level. It moves forward until reaching the door to the JINN's flat. Then, It simply stations Itself to the left of the door as we view it. And there It remains; still, silent and unseen. Its pulsating energy now absent. It awaits the cleaner.'

The BG "froze" the image, even as his audience pondered as to what he meant by 'cleaner'. After the briefest pause, BG pushed a button on his remote control. The screen sprang into life again, displaying more film of the front of the Library. It was now exactly nine AM. Just in time to see a large black van pulling up and disgorging women of a certain age. BG, facing the screen, explained.

'Behold, Cissie's army; of cleaners, that is. They make their way up and into the Library to go forth and clean. Only Cissie will go to the third floor. She's the only one assigned and trusted to attend to the JINN's flat. So, it is she alone we follow.'

In a moment of BG pausing, a hand went up, and he responded to what he assumed would be a request. He was correct. It was the Deputy Prime, asking about the reference to Frankenstein. BG obliged.

BG:

'Well, madam, I suppose a brief change of subject is no bad thing. I was referring to a particular similarity between Frankenstein and his Creation and the JINN and her 'creation'. How Frankenstein had turned against his creation, disowning it, wishing it dead. As to the JINN, she had created a terrifying, one time only killer: Blogges.

After he had served her need, she, with others, continued to learn as much about him as he cared to reveal, then, however good her intention, abandoned him; putting him on ice, almost literally.

Actually, into a prolonged Cryogenic Slumber. Partly in the hope of it reducing his memories and nightmares of the nights in recalling the horrors of his killing of Tregora. Albeit for different reasons, two creators deserting their creations. Ironic, don't you think?'

Before anyone could answer, BG turned back to face the screen, pressing his remote control as he did so. No one interrupted again.

Once more the film continued, as did the BG.

BG:

'And so we see Cissie coming out of the lift at the third floor, pulling her little cleaning trolley behind her. You can see the red mass of the Ethereal where last you saw It, and quite still.

Be aware of Cissie as she moves towards the front door of the JINN's flat. Not the slightest indication that she is aware of anything untoward as she reaches the door, unlocks it and opens it wide to the left. Now observe as the Ethereal follows in behind. No reaction at all from Cissie who, once in, along with her little trolley full of cleaning materials, turns and closes the door behind her. Also, of course, It now also being in the flat.

In the few seconds of viewing remaining of the entering, we also see the Ethereal moving wide and past the lady and onward into the flat, as a totally unsuspecting Cissie closes the door.'

BG "froze" the image and he turned to face his audience.

'We interviewed Cissie the following morning, not revealing what had befallen the JINN. The dear lady only confirmed what we knew. We had also viewed her as she left the flat almost two hours later. The Ethereal had remained in the flat'.

With that said, the BG once more turned to the screen as he operated the screen, bringing the images back to life, as he continued to narrate.

'It was now evening, dark, the time on the screen registering as seven-thirty PM. The JINN returning from her busy, not to mention rewarding day.'

The BG noted, as he pressed on his remote control, that 'they' were skipping forward to the third floor, as the JINN was now stepping out of the lift on the third floor.

Again, the BG "froze" the picture and turned to the audience, who remained still and mute.

Final Curtain Call Unseen:

'From this point, I'll be briefer still. Time, as said, is against us, as this Brief approaches conclusion, and I believe it to be honestly positive at the close. This shall be, as I will demonstrate, by showing a most potent weapon now at our disposal.

I start with the second death first. When I call out 'SHIELD', I will mean your eyes from the screen. Do not delay when I call out.

As the JINN moves to her flat door, like Cissie before her, note there is no display of concern, being unaware of anything untoward. She unlocks door, opens it, enters, closes it and, as far as we're concerned, her final curtain call with her killer, is unseen, unrecorded. We now turn to the Ethereal'.

Once more the BG faced the screen. The audience had become aware that the BG had been talking a little faster, a certain aspect of drama in his voice, although politely muted. He then pushed a button on his remote control and the screen sprang into active action. Being dark, there wasn't too much to see, save the lights from within the Library.

It was then it happened.

Out of the revolving door came that strange formless, faceless mass of red energy. In a few seconds the mass was pulsating. As It did so, the BG called out: 'Note the substation'.

The aforementioned small structure was beginning to display a light, pulsating red through the brick and edges of the metal grid and the edges of the door.

The red mass had now glided its way down the steps of the Library, turned to its left, the right as one viewed the screen, so facing the substation. It then began to glide at a pace. The BG called out again: 'Be ready!'

Then the pulsating red mass seemed to be getting both taller and wider, as the red energy from the substation radiated even further and brighter. And then, the greater mass that was the Ethereal, propelled Itself forward, seemingly jumping and lunging forward and into the red energy emitting from the substation, as the BG yelled out, whilst shielding his own eyes: 'SHIELD!!'. All in the room did so; audience, Watchers and the SASO Colour Sergeant all. There was a violent flash of intense, bright red light, seemingly exploding from the screen, which no one actually saw full on.

A few moment of silence, then all looked to the screen, uttering various sounds of anger, amazement, and not a little fear, save the hardened Colour Sergeant, Watchers and the BG amongst them. He looked to the screen, as did the others, now in confusion as much as anything. The BG "froze" the picture on the screen, not that there was much to see. It seemed some were watching out from the Library windows, the substation all but wrecked.

Of the red mass that had crashed forward and into it, nothing. It was dead and gone. Just like a spontaneous combustion of energy. Of human form?

The Ethereal wasn't human as such, just pure energy. So, one mass of energy consumed by another. Just another form of Kamikaze. If, as believed, these 'Ethereals' came with evil intent, they were certainly hostile. No surprise there. Somewhere, in a secret location, the Corporeal Self of one secured in a deep freeze, bust into Spontaneous Human Combustion. Within a few minutes, only a small mound of ash remained of what had been the husk of a once human being: Joseph Blogges.

Had those within the Library had their attention drawn to the great flash? It was not of itself the attraction alone. What those in the Library were also drawn to was the horrendous, prolonged human scream at the moment of the "explosion". Something the CCtv cameras did not, could not register.

The BG faced his audience, standing tall, straight and with a certain self-satisfied grin of darkest humour; but it didn't last. Someone was absent from the room: Colonel Evan Tomms.

The BG carried on regardless, addressing the small group of still silent and confused onlookers, who were seeking comfort as well as explanation. The BG obliged once more.

'What you've just witnessed, Prime Minister, ladies and gentlemen, is a rare sight indeed. The death of an Ethereal, and by suicide no less. Waste not a tear,' twas that bastard that killed the JINN, of whom I speak.

When any incident takes place in or around the Library, Watchers spring into action. Most go through the building to find out what's amiss and why. The two senior Watchers are charged with going straight to the JINN's flat to make sure she's okay. On this occasion it was not to be so.

They found her in her large, well-appointed study. Nothing, save one item, was out of place. An armchair, placed directly in front of the JINN's desk, facing directly to her. It was empty, of course. As a whole, the flat was immaculately Cissie clear, clean and sparkling, which was more than could be said for the deceased occupant in the seat behind the desk.

In the postmortem that followed, it was found that there was a small burn in her jumper, quite high on the chest. It turned out to have been an electric charge straight into her body, directly on to her pacemaker, frying its internal workings. The current had gone along the wire and so into her heart, stopping it immediately; for all eternity.

The Ethereal had known well Its human anatomy as regards heart placement and pacemaker. It should be recorded that the JINN's youthful look, along with her physical energy, belittled the fact she was 76 if she was a day.

Something more. The JINN and her killer had been together for some two hours, seemingly in a face-to-face exchange of one sort or another. Why, and about what?'

The BG was beginning to get a queasy feeling about it all. A single word flashed across his mind: conspiracy.

In the immediate moment, another and collective sense prevailed: a reverential, stunned silence from all, which in spite of his ever increasing dark thoughts, the BG allowed himself to silently appreciate.

Then the continuing process of guiding the Briefing to a conclusion. First, another grim disclosure of facts, and a hoped for positive and upbeat ending.

The BG went on to inform the others that the postmortem tended to acknowledge that the JINN's death had been relatively painless, peaceful; all things considered. If so, why?

Had she been known to the Ethereal, a colleague past, perhaps? The BG softly informed the gathered that it was almost a certainty that the great Lady has been murdered by the Ethereal Self of her own creation: the manufactured killer, Joseph Blogges. Other questions now crowded in, and the BG voiced them. How many of these bastards were there, from where, controlled by whom, and for why? Once more, the 'c' word flashed through his mind. Enough. Sufficient unto the moment.

The BG took a deep in-take of breath, as he turned off the big screen, instructing a Watcher to turn the lights full up in the room. It was then he realised Colonel Tomms had not returned. Still, to all intents and purposes, the main Briefing was over. However, the BG knew well the benefits of sending the audience on their way in a positive, happy frame of mind, although happy wasn't quite the word he had in mind.

As he turned and faced his audience, with a smile on his face, there was a marked, audible display of release of collective tension. For his part, the BG called John Smith to him, enquiring as to where Colonel Tomms had gone. He was informed that there had been a problem at AMOURAE, that he needed to attend to. The BG privately knew he'd had the man promoted too fast. No good gesture goes unpunished!

The BG accepted the reason, but was not happy about it. He instructed Smith to see the Prime Minister and his entourage safely to their cars when the Briefing was concluded.

The final item of the Brief was one the BG was quite looking forward to.

Splat and Zap!

The BG turned and nodded to the SAS Omega Colour Sergeant, smiling as he did so. In response, the seemingly immovable NCO moved into action. He knew just what to do.

As the BG began to explain to the assembled, the Colour Sergeant moved to the oversized hold-all, unzipped it and began to extract the content.

BG:

'Where possible thus far, I have exercised a certain light-hearted, flippant self, attempting to sooth many a troubled mind. I hope it succeeded, if only in part.

However, I now introduce you to a grim but necessary item; a weapon that kills; specifically Ethereals. First some definitions, so there are no misunderstandings as regards labels.

The 'Corporeal' being is you and I. Our physical Selves. A 'Separate' is a Corporeal being who can bring forth from him, or herself, their inner being. That's to say' the energy that courses through their body, which includes the brain, therein the psyche. Simply put, the mind. This released energy is referred to as the 'Ethereal'. It is this we seek to kill. Just as one that killed the man Tregora, and later took the life of our beloved JINN. Ethereals can also, it seems, bring out of themselves what might be referred to as 'doppelgangers' of themselves; carbon copies if you will.

As said, we have learnt a great deal from the Tregora killing, ironically, with much input from the late Joseph Blogges, amongst others. As to the mass of written reports, statements and the input of our many and varied experts, matters electrical. From this, we have produced the LGTR: The Laser Guided Taser Rifle. Only, this 'taser' is some three hundred times more powerful!'

There were murmurs in the gathering. One of the ladies appeared to have a tear in her eye. Another, a gentleman, whispered the words 'Dear God'.

To the BG, such fell on deaf ears, as he continued on

'We read that Tregora had let out an unearthly scream as he made his way some thirty feet or so into the back wall of his inner sanctum, courtesy of the Ethereal Blogges. There was no way he could have screamed, as he was Hell bound before he began his brief journey, already being stone dead and somewhat dismembered.

It seems one of his terrified thugs, most likely Hannibal, had fired a taser gun at what he thought was in front of the Butcher of Europe. It would have had little effect, as the fifty or so thousand volts would have been little more than urination in the face of a hurricane. Please forgive the crudity of my analogy. I mean compared to the vast amount of electricity that was within the Ethereal mass. As it has transpired, something in the order of three hundred thousand volts.

What we did learn was, that even with such a meager amount of electricity fired into It, It expressed some degree of pain. That was our starting point, and the beginning of the conceiving of the LGTR. And our hypothesis was also correct, as the spectacular demise of the JINN's murderer has since proved.'

At this juncture, the content of the hold-all had been removed and placed alongside the hold-all. On the face of it, a fearsome piece of armory. The Colour Sergeant had then stood back from the table and assumed the At Ease position, and the BG had moved forward and picked up the item in an expert manner, thanking the Colour Sergeant as he did so.

'And this is the weapon referred to, and very specifically made to kill Ethereals. Don't worry, it has not been set. Note I didn't say loaded, as it fires only electric bursts.

Such is its power, and of a danger even to expert and able users, they have to wear covering that would have done Darth Vader justice, and improvements re development continue'.

Absolute silence, as none dared to speak. The BG gave a slight smile of private satisfaction. Balance of seriousness restored. He continued on.

'Our more inventive grunts have given it another name: the 'Splat'n'Zap' Gun. Who said our soldiers didn't have a poetic streak!

This item is obviously larger, thicker than any normal rifle, but still light. Made of a special industrial plastic. It has a sort of electric power-storing, mini-substation in front of the trigger unit which generates the electric current. There is other piece of man-created magic in this weapon, but that remains totally Top Secret.

The trigger has a two-squeeze movement. The first squeeze releases a thin jet of bright red, sticky liquid that can travel up to fifty feet. The second squeeze, that can only function after the first, fires off something akin to an arrow-like burst of electricity, guided via the laser beam. There are no wires involved, rather a straightforward lethal charge.

You might like to know also that electricity travels at the speed of light, almost six hundred and eighty miles a second. Mind you, the electrons, stable, sub-atomic particles, are a tad slower.

Also, if you're wondering, a taser sends out its electric shocks via a thin electrical wire, whereas a laser stun gun administers such a shock by direct contact. Needless to say, the LGTR is in a different league and, as noted, of which some details are strictly top secret; even to you illustrious people.

Even so, a few more basic details to whet the appetite of anyone interested in such matters.

One last thing as regards to the nature of this item. It is a weapon, designed to kill what some are already referring to as a new species of humankind. For us, the Military, and those charged with directing it in protection and defence, I simply repeat a Military maxim: 'The best method of defence is ATTACK!'

And that, Prime Minister, ladies and gentlemen, is how we intend to take on any more Ethereals. We believe that, as said, the best form of defence IS attack … and **KILL!**' And just to clarify, when any human being is out of its Corporeal body, becomes Ethereal; a pulsating red mass of pure energy, and not, as we know it, *human*.

There was a restrained silence, which once more pleased the BG. He then decided a little more description wouldn't go amiss, so continued to do so.

'As stated, the LGTR is constructed of a heavy duty plastic, yet is extremely light.

It has two barrels, the one over the other.

The top one, coloured red, is both the electronic lazer tracer, and the means of ejecting a thin, bright red liquid, of some viscosity: it sticks to its target! If the marksman has judged the basic area where he believes an Ethereal is located, he employs the first squeeze of the trigger, so sending out the liquid at high velocity. Oh yes, you'll observe that the butt of the rifle is also painted red. That's because it is also the container for the liquid.

If he's found his mark, the marksman performs the follow-through squeeze and, through the lower barrel, coloured black, is fired the burst of highly charged electrical particles that enter into the Ethereal. As was seen with the JINN's killer, Ethereals do not fare well against high-powered voltage!

These highly charged bursts of electricity can melt solids and, where living matter is concerned, Man or beast, can fry it or them alive, not to mention possibly "exploding" of same.'

Silence descended once more, like a cloud of embarrassment. Not in the BG's case. After all, he *was* a soldier. The SASO Colour Sergeant had remained rock steady in his At Ease stance.

As the BG went on, it was clear that he seemed, momentarily, just a tad tired and tested to a degree of bored by the subject, not to mention the small audience as a whole, save for his Prime Minister. It was almost time to wrap up, but not before he had related the sad tale of the raging bull.

BG:

'In closing, Prime Minister, good people, I should point out that this rifle has been tested to the full, and not found wanting. On one of the MOD farms, a raging bull charged one of the SASO marksmen being trained in the use of the weapon. When the beast was but a matter of yards from the unflinching marksman, he fired, so first dropping the beast before it had progressed a foot further. Even before it hit the ground, it also "exploded" into flames'. Not unlike the JINN's killer.'

The audience, the Prime Minister included, did not respond to the grim little gem at all, unless you believe the silence that followed was appreciation enough.

For the BG it was enough. He suddenly seemed re-energized, clapping his hands as he called out to no particular Watcher in particular.

'That's all. Full lights, release the lockdown on the door! Watchers, attend our guests, escort them to their cars. To me, John Smith. Colour Sergeant, bag up the Splat'n'Zap', please. Return it from whence it came. A quick word, Prime Minister'.

The last request had been in a more respectful tone, as the BG moved to the Prime Minister, who now had John Smith at his shoulder. The three men stood apart from the others present.

The BG whispered to his Prime Minister that John Smith would see him and his people to their cars, and that a memory stick containing the just completed Briefing would be delivered to him at Downing Street by early evening at the latest, by courier from the Library, and in time for the pre-arranged COBRA meeting.

Just before John Smith moved his charges away towards the door, the BG moved over to the table, picked up his Briefing notes, moved back to Smith, handing the notes to him, whilst also taking his arm and whispering something to him. In fact, instructing Smith to arrange getting the notes to the Library ASAP. Also, giving a grim smile as he did so, instructing the man to find out the *real* reason why Colonel Tomms had buggered off, like a fugitive in the night.

That was it. This particular game, set and match was done. The question was, who won?

Within a few minutes, the room was clear, leaving the BG to contemplate on what had transpired. Within a matter of minutes, it happened.

John Smith had returned to the room, seemingly somewhat concerned, but in control. He requested the BG to follow him without delay. Before the BG could ask why, Smith had turned and left the room, his BG immediately following behind.

Truths Revealing

In moments, the BG was at John Smith's side, giving softly spoken words of instruction, support and encouragement.

BG:

'Relax, John. Walk at my side, slow pace, steady and assured.'

It worked. John Smith did so, smiling. He was more assured, because for him, 'the man' was at his side, mentally as well as physically. Even the sight Smith had beheld but minutes before seemed less than it had been.

It was a long corridor they walked, but the BG could clearly see some others outside a door on the left side.

As they got closer, the BG could see three SASO soldiers, one an officer, on the opposite side to the door, and two Watchers either side of the door. As the BG and John Smith got closer, the SASO men came to Attention, the officer saluting.

As the BG returned the salute, his touched his jacket, reassuring himself that his very special mobile 'phone was present and correct.

As they came to the door, the BG gave the Watchers a nod of acknowledgement, whilst also instructing for the door to be opened. His voice, commanding as always, was also calm and sotto voce. Not at all barrack square.

The effect on the Watcher who opened the door was just what the BG wished; a smile and acknowledgement of the command given.

The door was pushed open hard and fast, with the result that it opened inward and fully back to the left side. In a moment, the BG had strode in, looking immediately to his right as he entered the room, giving John Smith another, softly delivered instruction, smiling as he did so.

'Stay close to me, young man.'

Even as he spoke, the BG's superb mind was taking in what he saw. The end wall to the right was all glass. A mirror, left to right, bottom to top. Seemed a bit out of place to the BG's thinking, rather OTT.

Even as he viewed it, he was taking in what was reflected in it, to the setting at the other end of the room. A seemingly comfortable easychair, complete with arms, and quite empty. To the left and right of it, and at the back, Watchers. Standing to the right, and a little to one side, an SASO man, revolver drawn and at the ready.

Of course, now BG could also see his own reflection, and those of a somewhat confused John Smith, along with both the Watchers and the SASO officer in close attendance.

JOHN SMITH:

'Behind you, sir,' the young man respectfully prompted, as he had tapped his superior on the arm.

The BG turned around to face the other end of the room. His look did not change, but his mind and thinking was in dramatic re-set, as he spoke gently to his unofficial guide in the moment.

BG:

'Stay by me, John Smith, don't be afraid, for ghosts do not exist, only damned Corporeals and Ethereals!'

As he'd spoken, the BG had walked at a steady, even pace towards the other end of what was a more than average sized room. His look was neutral, almost bland. As he got close to the chair, the Watchers and the SASO soldier, came to Attention. The BG discreetly signaled for them to remain At Ease.

And then the BG was at the chair, staring down at the occupant, who seemed to be laying back, in something akin to repose.

The BG stooped down and first lightly touched the occupant's left cheek, then checked for a pulse at the neck, also the left side; both right side for the occupant of the chair. The BG seemed to have his hand at the neck for an unusually long period. He then withdrew it, stood up straight and addressed himself softly to John Smith, but loud enough for all in the room to hear.

BG:

'Pulse and natural body heat at least half they should be. In his present state, exactly what I'd expect. Mister Smith, I give you Colonel Tomms, who, methinks, is your first face-to-face Corporeal.'

Whilst John Smith was familiar with Tomms, he'd had no idea the Colonel was also a Corporeal. The BG completed the introduction.

BG:

'Colonel Tomms, I give you Mister John Smith'.

The Brigadier gave a still somewhat confused Smith a cheery smile as he turned to address all present in the room, whilst also reaching into his jacket pocket and extracting his rather special mobile 'phone. Several black and numbered buttons and a single bright red one.

'Gentlemen, for those still confused, I give you Colonel Evan Tomms. Head of Amourae and, as it turns out, also a Corporeal, Ethereal and a traitor! Hence you can't see his reflection in the mirror, as his Ethereal Self is absent.

As he'd spoken, the BG had pressed the red button on his mobile and, in a few moments, spoke into it.

'Robert, it's started. It's curtains up! Colonel Tomms is one of them; a Corporeal, and a bloody traitor. Christ knows where his Ethereal's buggered off to. Get LGTR squads to Downing Street, Parliament and Buck Palace pronto. Defend the flag, Bobby, pass the ammunition and God bless the JINN!'

With the last sentiment expressed, the BG tapped the red button and replaced his 'phone back into his jacket. He was on fire, yet as calm as the proverbial English officer and gentleman. Well, perhaps just a tad excited. One of the Watcher's approached him.

WATCHER:

'I think you should know, sir, as we were looking for the Colonel, at Mister Smith's instruction, we came to this door. As I moved to grab the handle, it sort of sprung open before I could. Although I'm sure I wasn't touched as such, I'd swear blind *something* rushed past me.'

BG:

'Which way, Watcher!'

The Watcher gave a little nervous laugh as he answered.

WATCHER:

'Couldn't say, sir, as I didn't see. Wait a minute, I thought someone had bumped into somebody by the exit, just down there a bit, sir.'

BG:

'What's immediately outside, Watcher?'

The Watcher thought for a moment, then, looking both surprised and anxious, gave answer.

WATCHER:

'It's the special parking space for VIPs, sir'.

BG (Grasping the significance of the answer):

'The PM's party? The Prime Minister!?'

WATCHER:

'Yes, sir!'

BG:

'God help us now, for it begins. Still, it is the hour we must first confront'.

A WATCHER:

'But where and who first, sir!?'

BG (Moving towards the exit door)

'To the barricades, to Downing Street. These Unseen, this Ethereal, is out to strike at our heart. **It**, is after Its prime target, and to kill it: The **PRIME MINISTER!!**'

END GAME

Of Nature, what to note, save beautiful, wondrous, awesome and fearful in her moods. Not to say mysterious. Also, staunch guardian and defender of her own child: Mother Earth.

As the BG and those that followed approached the particular exit from the MOD, they became aware of a darkness through the windows beyond their confines. Odd, the day had been fine when they had first entered.

As they ran out of the building, they saw for themselves how the sky above was turning day into night. They also became immediately aware of a powerful wind.

As the BG called for his men to make to their vehicles, a flash of lightning filled the sky, followed by a clap of thunder that seemed to echo throughout the world.

Most about the BG were hardened, military men, and simply accepted what obstacles were put before them, by Man or Nature. Mind you, the BG was taking it all in, analyzing and trying to fathom it. This was no ordinary day, mode of weather. All seemed in some sort of reverse, and at considerable speed. God's work or the Ethereals?

And then they were off, in pursuit of the Ethereal, and in defence of Prime Minister, God and country; and as always, the BG leading the charge.

Back in the MOD, in the room where Tomms' Corporeal Self still sat still and all but alone, save for two Watchers acting as sentinels, down at the mirror end, as they had no wish to look at the occupant of the chair for any longer than was necessary.

By now, heaven, in all its thunderous might, shook in anger at that which sought to usurp it, do harm to her child, Mother Earth, and her children upon it. It also, occasionally, displayed shield and sword, in the form of its sheets and jagged "spears" of lightning's fire. Above all, the rain that now swept, ever powerfully, all before it, yet seemed to enfold the small convoy that hastened it way to Downing Street, with gently cupped hands.

In the lead Rover, the BG was still trying to provide himself with a mental order of what was taking place. Also, watching out for a somewhat concerned John Smith at his side. The BG looked to him, smiling.

BG:

'Hang on, John Smith, this all too early a night may have started, but it's far from finished!'

John Smith flashed a nervous smile at his commander, whom he believed would be his shield, no matter what. After all, he was 'just a glorified civil servant clerk, not a hare'em, scare'em Military man. But he was right, the BG would shield him. It was his way.

They were now only a short distance from Downing Street. What would be there, what would they see? Would they be too late, or would the SASO men be equal to the hour?

And then, for the BG, the hour had arrived, as their driver swung a hard left and then a right into the world-famous street.

The BG looked hard, trying to spy the situation in the dark, rain swept street before him. He could barely see in front of him. He was able to see two SASO men, but the power of wind and rain held them back against the number Ten Downing Street side, and unable to raise their very special rifles. Ahead, the BG could see Number Ten, and the lights within.

He quickly called a special number on his mobile, and, speaking in a reasonably calm voice, a command, having first identified himself: 'Get those fucking lights out; please!!'

The lights went out: immediately, somewhat to the amusement of both the BG and the other occupants in the Rover.

And then they saw it, coming from the far side of the Street. It: the Ethereal out of Colonel Tomms Corporeal body. Above and all around it, crashing rain, with occasional sheets and forks of lightning.

What the BG, and all with him, were witnessing was a true, awesome clash of the titans; and in which they would play no part. Ethereals Light, against Ethereals Dark.

The BG made to get out of the Rover, but found himself pinned back by a force beyond his comprehension, as were those with him, and the SASO soldiers in the Rovers and Jeeps behind him. For but a fraction of a moment, the BG and all who sought to join the fight, were being held and kept safe behind an unseen hand Divine.

The Ethereal was now a glowing, pulsating red mass, emitting from its whole, steaks of electricity, in the form of "spears" and sprinklings of star-like explosions. Closer to Number Ten. Christ, It was nearly at the door!

Then, in a blinding flash, the mass simply blew up. It lit up the surrounds, lit up the heavens, that it had both challenged and defied.

And then followed a deathly silence, as the canopy of darkness began to immediately recede, and God's light once more began to reclaim His skies. Ceased also, the rains. As the light of day became more evident, bemused, unsure but relieved soldiers, the BG as much as any of them, and not forgetting John Smith, gave relieved smiles and thanks; to whom most were not entirely sure.

As a few, including the BG, got out of their vehicles, the Brigadier General was on his special 'phone once more, instructing those in Number Ten to turn their lights on. In a moment, they were.

As the BG drew closer to Number Ten, he looked down and saw it; a large red patch scorched into the paving stones, just feet from the famous door. What he had yet to be informed of, was back in the 'mirrored' room in the MOD, Colonel Tomms' Corporeal Self had, without warning, and sans any noise to speak of, self-combusted into a small pile of ashes on the seat of an otherwise untouched, unmarked chair.

As he approached, the door to Number 10 opened and the BG found himself facing his Prime Minister. He offered forth good news.

BG:

'We've won the battle, sir, although I don't fully know how or why.'

The BG gave a rueful smile as he stood to one side, pointing to the paving stones just outside the door. The PM gave a look of mild surprise, then, before returning into the premise, patted the BG's chest gently and reassuringly, as he gave an answer he seemed to believe was both true and absolute.

PM:

'Twas Divine rain and Heaven's fire that slew *this* beast, Brigadier General'.

end

Yurei

A call from the Ethereal Side

The Captain entered the large, starkly bare room. The ten high-backed chairs behind the specially constructed, semicircular table and, a few similar chairs around the far wall were the extent of the furniture to the far right. Several feet from the front of the table, a lectern, behind which a simple, straight-backed chair. Next to that, to the right, a small table, upon which a glass and a carafe of water.

To the surprise of the Executives, the Captain, sans any documents or the like to hand, made straight to the front and centre of the great table. As she viewed her bosses, she mentally, silently spoke an observation:

'Behold, those who wallow in the collective illusion of masculine power!'

The nine Executives made their own private, mental and individual observations.

The lady was about five ten, looked like the late Marilyn Monroe with, literally, a figure to match, and was beautiful, Also, sans any make-up. In work she broached no sexism, and stuck simply to business, the military way. She also had been seconded to the Ethereal problem, from a branch of Military Intelligence, by The Agency, and attached to the Brigadier General. Following on from his mentor, The JINN, he had set up a unit especially to monitor the Ethereal. One thing, however, the 'unit' consisted of just two persons: Slaughter and the BG. That was before early morning of the day, when she received a 'phone call. Even so, now somewhat in doubt as regards its authenticity.

For her part, she didn't waste any time. When she spoke, it was like warm honey, laced in vinegar! A JINN in the making, perhaps? By the book, no messing. No question, she was the real deal.

She spoke in respectful manner, as a subordinate addressing her senior officers.

'Gentlemen of the Executives Division, I was to come before you to give details of my findings to date on what is commonly referred to as 'The Ethereal Business'. However, I come to report a different matter, but which involves the same subject matter.

Our BG sent me on a different assignment following something that has derailed me before I started on my original one for you, as I believe he had found someone else to fulfil your instructions. I believe they're better qualified than I to do so.

Just after eight this morning, I received a call on my conventional landline 'phone. It was a male voice. He simply said I should take a close look at the Japanese island of Itsukushima, as that was where Joseph Blogges had spent his supposed "lost" two years. The caller then simply cut off. The call had barely lasted a minute. I, of course, immediately contacted our communications unit, who informed me that no call had come through my landline 'phone. Simply put, it was a "ghost" call; none-existent'. I tried to contact the Brigadier, but couldn't. I was simply told he was not available. That I should make contact with the other Executives. Your good selves, sirs.'

An awkward silence followed, the nine executives just staring at Captain Susan Ann Slaughter, in disbelief.

Some whispered words were exchanged between a few of the Executives and then one addressed the Captain.

EXEC:

'Captain Slaughter, would you please be so kind as to go and sit in the chair by the lectern for a few minutes, so we can confer'.

The Captain smiled sweetly and did as requested.

A further five minutes passed, a 'phone call made by one of the Executives, further whispered conversation followed, some sort of conclusion arrived at. Then, another of the Executives, signaled the Captain to come forward once more. She did so. He addressed her with what could be described as soft compassion.

EXEC:

'I'm afraid the BG is indisposed, indefinitely, Captain'.

After a brief pause, he continued.

'Captain Slaughter, we'd like you to return to your home and await further instruction. Perhaps you should put any present or scheduled work you have on hold, as we believe your attention should be now focused solely on this Ethereal matter.'

That was it. Captain Slaughter, ever the good soldier, did as requested, returning home, with a muted, unexplained sense of loss.

That evening she received her orders via The Agency 'phone around eight o'clock. Her feelings after the call were mixed; of loss and excitement. Not the best of bedfellows. If only she'd known, that soon she would end up entering into the strange, fathomless heart of beings of The Fourth Kind: extra-terrestrial. Aliens. She, and any, knowingly or otherwise, who had encountered those of the Fourth Kind were, themselves, referred to as Human Beings of the Third Kind. She began to wonder if some so-called "experts", and recorders of the history of the madness, were in some way trying to connect heritage, lineage with what, by any sane definition would be seen and recorded as *aliens!*. Maybe trying to get on their good side, if they did take over the world!

Note: In the course of time, it became known that the Brigadier General had died suddenly in the early hours of the morning. Cancer. No other details available outside of the Executives. It was The Agency policy in action, whenever a senior individual died. Someone called it 'Silent Mourning'. The tag stuck.

Enter another Ethereal

Cameron Coach was young, fit, able and one of the latest batch of new agents to be coming off the production line. He was up and ready for it, and in a matter of months, he'd become a fully-fledged Agent.

Until then, he had to suffer the embarrassing title, to go with his already given Agency non du plume. As was the Agency way, he "lost" his real name when he was accepted into The Agency as a "Greenie" (a trainee) some three years before, He would keep his Agency name, Yurei, until his retirement or death; whichever came first. It was The Agency giver of non du plumes to new agency operatives who gave him the name, as he was back on the 'Y's list. It was, by happenstance, the Japanese word for faint or dim. Mind you, it also meant soul or spirit: even ghost.

What was to happen to him would be recorded on the CCtv system in the flatlet, dramatically changing everything.

Before the night was over, Coach Cameron, as his close friends called him, would have a nightmare like no other. The more so as it passed through nightmare in sleep into nightmare within the awakened sleep; half unconscious, half semi-conscious.

Came the early awakening hours of morn and he would, in reality, through another, become messenger and conduit of same as much as agent to be.

Without his realising or by direct, intentional involvement, it began with the process of metamorphosis, via Cameron exercising the Separate skills at his disposal, but of which he had no personal knowledge: bringing forth from his own Human Being of the First Kind to one of the Third kind (one who has encountered an entity not of this world), and as an Ethereal, via Transference (later called 'TEA-bagged' by another), so himself, by default, one of the Fourth Kind. This, by 'separating' his Ethereal Self from his Corporeal Self. As stated, it began in nightmare, and finished in the mire of a nightmarish reality of first semi-consciousness, then into full consciousness, ending in the comatose state.

As he began the process of waking, he felt another Self moving within him, then could only watch on in disbelief, whilst entering into an overwhelming sea of pain, as he witnessed some other form of life slowly rising into the sitting position from within him. From there, seemingly to raise Itself completely from its host being, as It glided to and off the foot of the bed, turning to look down at his host Self, whilst It assumed the standing position.

Cameron Coach viewed all clearly through continued waves of unspeakable pain, staring at what could be termed, by any other description, as his own doppelganger. His own, physical self.

And then the pain drained from him, as he also felt that his body was now *empty*, without content, as if his inner Self had departed from him, which it indeed had.

It would return in due course, after delivering knowledge to an unsuspecting Major.

'Soon the truth of all'.

And then, at speed, it dissipated from view.

Silence had followed.

Before the day was done, Watchers had arrived, as the trainee agent of The Agency had been filmed on his flatlet CCtv. They found the young man still in bed, in deepest sleep, soon to be diagnosed as a comatose state.

All about was normal. Perhaps with one exception. His bedclothes were all but redundant, more off the bed than on.

Cameras, Action!

The Executives Division were duly informed, as was a certain Army Captain, who'd been secretly seconded, by them, into the late Brigadier General's relatively newly formed E-Unit within The Executives Division, but the brainchild of the JINN. In truth, the Unit consisted of just two; Slaughter herself and the BG. It was at times such as these that Captain Slaughter wished for the wisdom and a comforting arm to guide her: from her late mentor.

Captain Slaughter was already familiar with the Ethereal problem. For the record, her full name was Susan Ann Slaughter. The Ann bit was to make her initials SAS; as her late father had been in the world-renowned Regiment, back in the day. To her friends, she was nick-named SASee. Work it out.

The Captain was somewhat surprised to see a full Agency team in the small flatlet when she got there. She questioned the speed and efficiency of it all. One of those present explained that "Greenies" in the last six months of their training period were moved into Agency flatlets. Amongst other things, it meant a certain discipline be met by them; the curtailing of any sexual exploits they might have had in mind.

This requirement backed up by the CCtv system in each flatlet. One of the last, though still important hurdles, would-be agents had to endure: Discipline of Self!

She also noted all were standing away from the stricken trainee's bed, with just one man next to it. The Captain thought she'd seen him somewhere before; he was one of the Executives. He had a hand mirror and was holding it over the comatose occupant in the bed. He beckoned the Captain over, inviting her to observe the reflection in the small mirror. There wasn't one, and the Captain nodded her acknowledgement of what that meant. She also put a hard, direct question.

CAPTAIN (CAPT):
'Where is the bastard, sir!?'

The Executive, Head of the HR Division, sighed as he stood up straight, replacing the small hand mirror back into his pocket. He then pulled out an official looking envelope and handed it to the Captain, who found herself looking down to her senior; she being five feet ten, he barely making five six. But, he had presence and authority, in both body language and voice. Also, of course, the power of the full Executive behind him.

He was also old school, smiling and courteous in his manner. However, his words were straight, concise, like bullets of command. He moved away from the bed and guiding the Captain away also, until both were isolated in a corner of the room.

EXEC:

'The envelope contains your written instructions. Here's the verbal version. You're moving to an Agency flat in Whitehall. It will be your hub until this Ethereal madness is dealt with. Now you go home and sort out any personal matters you may have. You'll be picked up tomorrow or the next day, depending on events. Be ready. You're to continue collating and monitoring all information appertaining to this nightmare, including this latest episode. You will be given all assistance, including what others may come up with.'

With that said, the Executive began to lead the Captain towards the door, whispering to her as they went.

EXEC:

'You're being promoted to the rank of Major, to give you more clout.

Captain Blaine is taking over your old command, with your present assistant, Sergeant Alison Varney, being his aide. It has been decided that you're of the right stuff as regards helping to sort out this madness. You'll answer to the (replacement) Brigadier General, who knows well his business.'

The Executive guided the newly promoted Major out of the room, closing the door after them, leaving both alone on the landing for a minute or so. He spoke again, sotto voce.

'When you get there, tomorrow most likely, you'll see a red 'phone and a new laptop in your temporary residence. The 'phone is a direct line to the Executive Division's information line, manned twenty-four-seven.

Both the 'phone and your laptop are programmed to your handprints, including your fingertips. So, both strictly for your use alone.

The person who comes to you tomorrow will be your guide and assistant. As a Watcher, he will be there to watch over and protect you, for who knows what the days are yet to present to us.'

'It wouldn't be one of the BG's "ladies", sir?,' probed the newly promoted Major, giving a slight mischievous smile. She wasn't nick-named Sasee for nothing.

The Executive's reply was brief, to the point and simply didn't broach response.

EXEC:

'No, child, but she is exceedingly able, and you deserve some good news, input'.

All things considered, the Major believed The Agency wasn't quite *that* heartless. Slaughter kept her air of calm, but it was clear confusion was still writ large on her face.

MAJOR:

'Sorry, sir, I'm still a little adrift'.

The Executive gave a sympathetic smile as he answered.

EXEC:

'As are we all, Major, with another Ethereal on the loose. Also a fine young man deprived of his inner man, and who knows, maybe his soul also. Not to mention our revered BG past.

Don't worry, Susan, I'll 'phone you tonight and give you more details. You have the full weight and authority of the Executives Division behind you, not forgetting the entire Agency. You shall not want for support and guidance.

In passing, best to be in civvies for this one, I think. That's when you move into your Whitehall flat, that is. Don't want to scare the natives! Up and at it, Major!'

That was it. Slaughter no longer feeling like a lamb being led to the slaughter. She felt strong, invigorated, knowing that the entire Agency was behind her. And, in spirit at least it would seem, the late BG himself.

There was also another waiting to enter the fray directly, the unknown 'other lady' mentioned . The lady in question being one Finola Flowers by name.

As the Executive had returned into the room, so Slaughter had started on her way down the stairs. As she did do, she saw one thing, thought another.

The former were the medical team on its way up to remove the stricken Agency trainee to a special medical facility. Of the second, of the BG, and one of his favourite calls to arms: 'Game on!'.

Slaughter was sporting a beautiful, delighted smile as she left the building, with those that observed left wondering why.

Why indeed?

An afterthought: how long before those that were tasked with wading through the BG's many personal papers would they come across, a brief, hand scrawled note by the man to himself. Not within his notes, but placed where one would least expect. It was like a little listing of immediate problems to be addressed. That the Ethereals were still evolving, and could, before too long, most probably fly; that their strength had increased tenfold; that soon they would be beyond sighting; filters or no. INVISIBLE to the naked eye. That detailed forensic examination of the red-stained paving stones outside Number Ten Downing Street, exposed two different DNAs; one belonging to the none lamented Colonel Tomms, the other of unknown origin: i. e. *alien*. His final words, writ large, being: 'God help us all!' There was an omission. The late Brigadier General did not know that the Ethereals could become doppelgangers as and when desired. Even so, he knew some of what was to be, but others, a Major and a new agent within The Agency, would be destined to hear and repeat the message and intent of the Ethereals of the Light.

Truth to tell, this particular written record would be secreted into the bowels of the Library, and in the 'FORBIDDEN' area, lodged between two locked document boxes, by the BG himself, there to gather dust, until someone else discovered them. Why? Upon instruction from some greater power, Ethereal in nature?

And who was to say that perhaps the BG was himself wasn't servant to that greater power? And much of his information had been secured by, let us say, 'a Flower' by name.

Same ballgame, different Captain: a Major!

Came the day, 9AM sharp, and a firm crisp knocking at a Major's door.

A voice called out. It was strong, commanding, yet somehow seemed young.

'Cab for Major Slaughter!'

It was indeed ' Game on'.

Truths told

The Major was standing and facing away from the door when the knock came. When she turned around, ready to move forward to open the door, she was stunned to find that not only was it open, but that a tall, good looking and very able young man was now inside, and also sporting a warm, cheery smile.

The biggest surprise for Susan Ann Slaughter was that she knew the young man, for she had seen him the previous day, and seemingly 'not himself'. It was the trainee agent Coach Cameron; agency name – YUREI. And yet the voice had sounded just like …

The major stood open mouthed in surprise, and then recovered herself and made to speak. Not fast enough. The young man made an exaggerated move with his right hand, moving it from left to right, seemingly in some sort of grand gesture of greeting. It was enough. The major passed into a beautiful, wakened sleep, whilst remaining standing.

And then she seemed to find herself in some other, unworldly world. The man, Coach Cameron, still stood before her, but himself seemed to be different, not fully in or with either himself or his situation. His eyes seemed to convey some other person, simply inhabiting the real Coach

Cameron's body. He was and was. His *sound* of voice and the choosing of the words he spoke confirmed this. The eloquence somewhat more pronounced. But not at all threatening. Indeed, comforting and embracing in some manner. Just like the deceased BG in some other time (and space!?).

CAMERON'S ETHEREAL SELF (Ce):

'My time is limited, and I have things to tell, reveal. I speak to you mind to mind, as you can also speak to me. Question only if you have to. To keep things simple, I shall use the terminology you apply to us, and within your own kind.

Your scientists are reasonably close in their time-space continuum concept. We are without names or labels. We simply are: Ethereals. Humans that see and communicates with us, seemingly referred to as Humans of the Third Kind. And, as you seem have so politely termed us, "Humans", of The Fourth Kind'.

The Ethereal gave to the Major a gentle, reassuring smile, wrapped in, as a parent might smile to its child, by way of comforting, putting it at ease. He continued on.

'Like all sentient beings, we are of both Light and Dark in our nature. Also, as you will gather from this, Humankind is far from alone in the vastness of existence.

As to how we came to be here, not so long ago, in your time measure, a number of us, myself included, fell through an unexpected fissure betwixt time and space.

A few of us entered into what you refer to as your universe, wherein that beautiful spherical ball of light and colour you call Earth.

No, I apologise, but he was beyond our reach. One day, cancer will cease to be. I promise.

It was a few of our Dark side who laid siege to your Downing Street. Your Prime Minster attributed your God as coming to the rescue, when, in fact, it was we from the Light side who did so; willingly. It served the purpose of we Ethereals of the Light, as we did not wish for those of the Dark to accompany us on the long and none too sure journey back to our own domain, so we killed them. They will bother you no further.

Of course not, we of the Light have nothing against you as a species. We wish you only well.

I am quite sure your God would have proved just as able to the hour. But, in truth, we thought it was the least we could do, having entered your world uninvited.

Yes, Yurei, A strange name, but typical civil servant mentality, you could say, as the giver of names was back on the Ys listing. It means faint or dim; but also soul or spirit: even ghost. I think young Coach has the highest potential, having both soul and spirit, and a certain way about him. As do you, Susan. Before I depart this interesting world, after the "storm", I shall gift to you both a higher mental and physical energy.

I believe that both you and Coach are destined for greater things, beyond the military and even beyond The Agency.

Soon enough, Susan. Even for us, it takes a little time to prepare such a storm. But fear not, for it is coming soon enough.

Returning to you and Cameron, you both have the drive for good, and at these turbulent times in this world of yours, such is to be guarded, encouraged and developed. Again, the least we Ethereals of the Light can do. It will begin for you and Coach Cameron when you both make known this experience you are both going through, and passing on the message I now convey to you. Although methinks that will not be necessary, as your 'Agency' has communication facilities enough and more.

Yes, I must own up and apologise, for it was I who led your people on a wild goose chase. I thought is best you be out of the way whilst we prepared to do what shall soon be.

Forgive me. Also, in passing, by 'we' I speak for all the Ethereals of the Light, at present on this globe of delight.

Also, I was in Japan, when your Joseph Blogges was passing through, on some matter or other. I bumped into him, by intended accident. In that, it transmitted to me the essentials of his person.

So, I borrowed his body one night, whilst he slept, using it has a host base so to speak. I went for a stroll, then returned. I then departed from my host, but not before giving to him certain means and ways, by way of the two gifts I shall pass into both young Coach Cameron and you. In truth, I have already done so, as you both shall be aware of in the course of time, once you both resume your normal lives; professionally and personally. As to the human, Nobel, one of our own was close to him at the time of his dying. He would have intervened, but decided, due to the man's mental state, it would not have served him well, and he had given us what we required. So, we allowed him to end his days.

Thank you, but any Ethereal, of the Light or Dark, can assimilate any language, any dialect, to any command of the language in question. I cannot claim any such skill alone.

You have some remarkable people. Your 'Executives' as a body, also, as individuals, both the late Brigadier General and, perhaps most of all, the lady you referred to as 'the JINN'. She was truly exceptional. Be that so, she betrayed one of our own, for which the sentence had to be death. It is our way.

Yes, you're very astute. To aid us maintain a certain anonymity, we were able to 'persuade' some of your people to assist, aid us to that end.

Do not be too hard on them. We are possessed of the ways and means to turn their minds to our way of thinking. And please note, I did not use the term 'bend'. Too crude. The gentle way is mostly the better way.

Yes, your people show remarkable abilities to adapt and improvise. The 'Splat and Zap' weapon being an excellent example, albeit rather crude and limited. However, as you will have noted, simply not capable of stopping the intent of either an Ethereal of the Dark, or Light for that matter.

Yes, again. Taking up the stained paving stones was very good, but we could have saved you the trouble. I'm afraid the taking of Tomms was natural for us; Dark to Dark as it were. The Colonel was not all that he seemed'.

To Major Slaughter, it was as if she were being hypnotically serenaded by the Ethereal, in the guise of Coach Cameron, but possessed of the voice of the BG passed.

And yet, one who was potentially her enemy, was charming, courteous and answering all the questions that she asked; mind to mind that is, for all the dialogue was in silence.

But, for how much longer, to what end?

The Ethereal "heard" the Major's concerns and stepped in once more.

'Do not fear, Susan. Coach Cameron is in exceedingly good health. As we speak, he is up on his feet, dressed in pajamas and dressing gown, explaining all to a few of the Executives and senior medical personnel, as I do to you now. He has more or less spoken my words, but for obvious reasons, they seem not to believe him, that he suffers from a malady of the mind. No matter, when the storm comes, they will understand what he has spoken. When you go to him, Susan, as you shall shortly do, you will confirm and support him in what he has said. I shall leave it to you to describe the nature of the storm to come, as Coach Cameron is about to try and do, as I am about to describe to you. Most probably, they will not believe him. Nor even you, when you are back at his side and also repeating what I will have told you. Your audience will, as they have done with Coach Cameron, declare that you suffer from the same malady as Cameron. No matter, they will believe soon enough, after the storm has past.

I assure you, Susan, Cameron is already realising the changes within him, and to the better. Sharper in mind, fitter in body. His thinking is clearer, more concise.

This is all down to boosting his mental and physical capacities. As said, you have also been accommodated in a like manner, as you will slowly realise, once I have departed this place, your world. Again, it is the least that I, we could do.

Ah yes, the perfect way in which to conclude.

The time frame I give will be in relation to each country upon this glorious globe.

The full fury of this storm to come shall not, in any way, touch or harm any living thing, Man, beasts, flora and fauna and all life and matter upon, above or beneath this beautiful globe of colour and light.

It will be as no other storm past, present, or ever in the future.

It will be the Cleansing of Humankind's collective mindset. Removing all thoughts of vanity, avarice, acts of violence of any kind, in mind or by deed. The storm will last for forty days and forty nights. In our time, that is. But, for but a day and night by your human measure of time.

Come the forty -first day, from dawn of the morrow in your time, the Cleansing will be complete.

How long this state of the new Eden in the mind of Man remains, will be determined by Man himself alone. Humankind that is.

To turn the human face from it will ultimately result in the removal of life, all life, from this most beautiful, life packed and giving globe you call Earth.'

Susan heard the words and, in a way that surprised her, understood the implication of them. Yet, she was still in a reverie of grace, in a room that did not echo to any sounds of the spoken word. Such was the way and command of the Ethereal.

'Forgive me, I almost forgot. Herewith, a description of this storm of which I speak, and of Humankind of the Fourth Kind, as your kind inclusively appear to refer to us collectively, *and, of course, 'ETHEREALS!'*

And so, he, It explained the nature of the storm.

'Prior to its beginning, there will be a Prelude to the overture. A gentle breeze. Those outside, in the open, shall hear it, but will not see or feel any physical manifestation of it.

Then they shall see what they will believe to be the illusion of the sky lowering, but will not be disturbed by it.

They shall see the materialisation of vast white clouds, which will thereafter become both heavy and grey in their look, then darkest dark.

Then, as the afternoon progresses within each and every land, the first distant sounds of thunder shall be heard. It will become louder, but not enough to bring fear, only the slightest hint of concern.

For the old, the infirm and the children, and the animal life, wild and tamed, all that shall be heard will be the gentle sounds of heaven's own lullaby.

However, for the adults of the lands, as the thunder increases, also too the sense of foreboding and fear. To them a sort of awakened sleep shall enfold them, so delivered by beings on high, of which you have no conception.

And then, as evening comes, so too the rain, also heaven sent.

And with it, the slow realisation that, even as it becomes heavier, it neither descends on people, or any other living thing. Nor even upon the ground, nor the earth nor seas of the world. A wonder to behold, but not to understand.

As the evening beckons, so wind and rain becomes more violent, high above the heads of all that lives. The wind sweeping across the lands, screaming like Hell's own banshees; the rain firing downwards, like billions of bullets fired from the sky over all the lands and seas of the world.

Yet, through all of this, seemingly Nature's rage, the oceans of the world to remain calm, reflecting like giant mirrors, the wrath unleashed above them.

Throughout, Man and Earth shall remain dry, untouched, unharmed. And nothing of their making damaged, in any way. Nor any living creatures of the Earth afeared or harmed.

And the Cleansing will continue as, out of normal sequence, heaven's fires arrive; in the form of lightning, in sheets and jagged daggers from on high.

In depth of night, greater still shall be the rage from above, as all life upon Earth is suspended, held within a void. None shall either see nor hear as the Cleansing of the world, and the minds of Man, continue until all is done.

And, on the forty-first day, in Man's time, in each country's time, dawn shall break, ushered in by a radiant golden sky, in each country's time.

The air and the seas throughout the world, clear, clean and cleansed.

And so, a modern Eden, inhabited by present Man. For how long, Mankind will decide. They shall choose, and by their own actions alone.

All we, Ethereals to you, ask is that you, Humankind, choose wisely.

To soil your lives, continue to kill, plunder and destroy, both yourselves and the very land you call Earth, and lay low all that is yours once more shall, as already stated, bring about your demise, and cast this Earth into everlasting darkness.'.

For just a moment, all about the Major seemed lost in darkness. Then all was light once more. Susan felt free, elated, almost delirious in delight, as the life before her, the Ethereal, as Cameron's own doppelganger, stood smiling at her happiness, enjoying also her moment of realisation of the moment.

And then the Ethereal lifted up its right arm, extending its hand, palms outward towards the Major's face, giving one final, beautiful smile, as it uttered soft, final, gentle words before leaving her in an instant: **'Softly at your side, we unseen tread'.**

And so it would be for the Major. A quiet, untroubled and, before too long, gentle conclusion to her Military life. Retirement and seclusion. Likewise, also for Coach Cameron; sans his Agency name. Removed, expunged from the record. Such were the ways and means of the Ethereals, through others.

And of the storm, what? Time passed by. Nothing particular. Was it to be, or not to be? More time passing. And then, when an afternoon came, so came the overture to the storm. The Ethereals had begun the process of cleansing, as they themselves departed.

end

'You are not alone'
By the time she returned to her office, her joyous staff had done the necessary to her uniforms in her wardrobe. Namely,

the "pips had gone and the St. Edward's Crown held pride and place: the insignia of a Major. And that was the only good news as such.

'Alone'

The belated storm had come and gone, and not so long past, and yet it had been as nothing witnessed before. And why the delay in its coming, when announced a considerable time before? And when it came and then passed, what of the stillness throughout the world; a calm in both Nature and Man, and was present still, but perhaps faint now more the echoes of Man and Nature past. Now the weather seemed almost its normal self, the first signs of human discourse becoming evident once more, albeit slight. Even so, more familiar winds and rains were as before, blowing hard through the lands, and soaking the residents of that land as and when.

And was it possible that the memories of the Ethereals past were fading; even doubted?

In an office within the great City that was London, a man swiveled his chair around, away from his desk, so he could look out of his window, musing on such matters. What a miserable sight he now beheld, and when the only view was that of Millbank, and so little a view of the Thames to see. And yet, as stated, there was a still and calm evident. Was this seeming peace on Earth and within the hearts of Men *real*, or just imagined? That was one thing the man in the office had been charged to investigate and finally lay to rest. All he had to work on were the memories and the recalling of others. It was, he'd thought, like trying to nail a dream to the wall of reality. And then, whose dream, and upon which wall? And what did it truly have to do with the usual world of the Intelligence Service, more used to the real, shitty and bloody world of spies, espionage and traitors?

The Man

The man questioning so was J, the first so designated Head of the entire British Intelligence Network, referred to simply as 'The Agency', and who now sat in his office within MI5. He hadn't even been able to secure an office with a window that provided a better view of the Thames, not to mention full sight of the gaudy MI6 building on the Albert Embankment, in which he had been offered an office, but declined, sticking with the more solid and stolidly boring look that was the MI5 building. For why such a choosing?

All wasn't as simple as it seemed. Some called the MI6 building 'The Bond building', after Ian Fleming's hero. All flash, bang and fantasy. Whereas, the MI5 building's unofficial name was the 'Smiley Building', after George Smiley, one of the great characters in the spy genre, and created by John le Carre in his 'Tinker, Tailor' novels. Also, far more down-to-earth, realistic and, dare it be said, slightly boring? The building that is, not the Le Carre novels!

And what of the reality of J and 'The Agency'?

From a sea cadet to able seaman and on to become an Admiral: a Rear Admiral, actually. He'd also spent two years in Naval Intelligence. Details not known. After which, on being informed he wouldn't make it to full Admiral status, he received a most unexpected proposition. To become the first official Head of 'The Agency'. In fictional terms, the equivalent of 'M' in the Bond books and 'The Controller' in the le Carre novels. And why 'J' in reality? It was in honour of 'The JINN'. And why not.

And as we're talking names, what was J's actual name? Whilst not divulging his surname, his first name was Vincent (or Vinh for short). Only his closest friends called him that, and no one in the professional world in which he moved and worked. It was either 'J' or 'Admiral'.

It should also be put on record that he was given a 'handle' when he entered fully into the cloak and dagger world of spies and espionage. That's to say, a knighthood.

And of his character, what? Certainly not like the Brigadier General, and not in the same universe as the legendary JINN.

Even so, outstanding in his way.

Calm, steady, in full knowledge and control of whatever brief he'd been given, and possessed of a good humour and, when necessary, both hard and cutting. When called for, he had a way of making even the strongest adversary cringe and capitulate. In look, not unlike the actor of old, John Mills, in military character. As a champion to a cause or for an individual, none better, truer and stronger. Even so, in light of this Brief, imagination limited and no philosopher he.

Yet all so said, he was a good choice to *manage* The Agency. Administrator supreme.

And returning to the moment, what was on his mind in that moment? What had been niggling away almost from the day he first took office in The Agency, which was not so long ago? Again, at the back of his mind, that single word:

ETHEREAL. Had all that had past been true, or some gigantic, collective storm in the mind of Man been told true? Had that "storm" really heralded the departure of the Ethereals of the Light, and also the death of the Ethereals of the Dark? Was the Earth at last free of the madness, or not truly possessed at all? And of the seemingly peace and calm of both Earth and Man, what? The parting gift from the Ethereals of the Light, perhaps? Could it have been so simple, complete and final? And what of Coach Cameron (Yurei) and Major Slaughter? Not so long ago, it seemed to have done for two outstanding members of the Agency. Let us simply say they were 'retired' early. And The Agency itself wasn't without blame in the affair. Were the Ethereals of the Light calling the tune, even to the end, and if at all?

Questions, questions. All was questions Wherefore bloody answers!?

Most would, eventually, be laid to rest, at least to a fair degree, by J and one other. Neither of them having being involved at the outset of the madness, only ever on the edge of it, but present at its probable ending. Essentially, outsiders both, but now, thanks to the late BG's* forward planning, charged with finally laying it to rest, whatever it was, or might have been. Even so, as intimated, two others within The Agency had experienced a direct encounter, coming face-to-face, in a manner of speaking, with a representative of the Ethereals; and so noted here in the plural. Both, a man and a woman had thereafter been shunted into 'retirement and quiet seclusion' and those that had been privy to what they in turn, had said, advised to forget the telling; by the behest of the Ethereals again, perhaps? Such was the state and situation when J became Head of The Agency. However, to begin, he had to soldier along on his own. He wanted a forensic overview of the whole Ethereal business, as BG himself had intended, and indeed, unbeknownst to all but a few, had set in motion. However, as Head of The Agency, there was only so much time J himself could give to it.

Even so, when the *BG died suddenly (cancer, and not verbally noted thereafter. The Agency version of 'silent mourning'), the second person in question found herself 'stepping up to the plate, seemingly not even knowing to whom to pass her findings. In the course of time, providence would provide for the two; J, and the woman, Flowers. Neither known to each other at the outset. Flowers seemingly to no one of note.

The rain continued to fall. The sound of it gently continuing to hit J's window, producing an almost soporific sound. One that could, so easily, lull one into a false sleep.

For a few moments, J looked at the little brown clay pot on his windowsill, in which a plant of some description rested. He didn't remember its name, but then he wasn't really into flora and fauna. It had been a gift from a little child of a friend he knew, so felt obliged to accept, display and attend it. But J was Hannibal Lecter, not Percy Thrower!

Once more, J swung his chair back around to face his desk and to continue reading various notes and papers relating to the Ethereal matter. Would he ever get to put it all into an acceptable context, narrative even, for his masters? Not to mention the two that had been so affected? After all, it was they who'd directly heard a possible representative of the Ethereals give account. However, not to J himself. He'd only heard second hand, and then through film alone.

Flowers From A Distance

As stated, what J also did not know, was that another had been studying the Ethereal problem, the patterns of it all, not to mention the overall affect it seemed to have on the Agency personnel in general.

When that 'other' heard, indirectly and by chance, that the new 'official' Head of The Agency and the first 'J', was somehow involved, *she* thought it time make herself known to him.

Being the late BG's one and only 'unit' in the 'E-Unit' he'd set up to focus on the whole Ethereal phenomena, she was all but invisible to just about everyone. Such was the world of spooks; the left hand not necessarily knowing what the right hand was about. Interestingly enough, this certain lady hadn't come on to the J's radar. That was about to change. Shortly, he was to hear, and eventually see first hand, the results of her labours over the last few years. Would also learn of the lady's remarkable gifts. Almost unreal.

Those, included her ability to befriend at a distance, and keep a professional distance. That she could detect flaws and defects in human relationships, behavior and potential dangers in same. Mind you, she had also received the benefit of access to certain extremely top secret documents and people; courtesy of the late BG, along with photographic evidence and most secret reports concerning those who had fallen foul of the Ethereals, or under their influence in some way.

Not to mention also, indirect and discreet assistance and advice from the few who felt that not enough involvement was present to resolve the business once and for all, and of the same view and resolve as the late BG. Conspiracy seemed not so far removed.

Without a doubt, the BG had chosen well; Finola Flowers was perfect to her calling; which included working in the outerlands of the Intelligence Service, prior to being secretly seconded into the BG's Ethereal Unit by the man himself and, in reality, being the one and only working unit, the BG notwithstanding, at the time of his death.

So, the moment she got wind of the 'J's interest, she made her move. She put a call through to the office of the Head of the Agency.

The Call

The call was taken by J's personal secretary, the redoubtable Agnes Plumb.

'The Plumb', as she was often referred to by J, was more than able to deal with any and all; be they high or low in status. The more so if they were also full of it. Hot air, that is. Although not renowned for her humour, she did possess a keen wit and turn of phrase, cutting or praising, as and when she deemed required or deserved.

When the caller gave her reason for calling, Plumb told her to hold on, and then referred her request, via the intercom, to J.

For his part, in a further moment of mental idleness, J had been perusing the top of his more than ample sized desktop. He liked it to be clear of clutter, but such was not so. Upon it, three 'phones; one red, the second white and the third blue. The first gave him direct and immediate access to the Prime Minister in Downing Street, along with MI 5 and 6; the second, for making and receiving calls both within the United Kingdom and overseas, the third for 'personal' use. All fitted with top-of-the-range, state of the art security facilities. Then there was the intercom box, pen and pencil holder, leather-bound writing pad folder and address book. Last, but by no means least, a neat little laptop. The printer was on a small table to J's right. An uncluttered desktop slowly becoming more and more cluttered.

The buzzing of his intercom brought him back to matters immediate. He pressed a switch and spoke.

J:

'Yes'.

PLUMB:

'A young lady wishes to see you most immediately, sir.'

J:

'And who might *she* be, secretary mine?'

The Plumb allowed the little barb to pass. There was a moment of silence, and then she gave answer.

PLUMB:

'Finola Flowers, sir. She says she worked for the late Brigadier General.'

J:

'Tell her to make an appointment like anybody else'.

Another brief pause, and then came the reply that made J sit up and take notice.

PLUMB:

'The lady has three Red Star clearance, sir. She also told me to mention a single word to you: ETHEREAL'.

Now J's attitude and manner changed completely; direct and commanding.

J:

'Get her in here fast, Plumb, and cancel my appointments for the day and any other business'.

Another brief pause, and then once more the Plumb's disembodied voice.

PLUMB:

'She will be with you within half-an-hour, sir, and she told me she will be bringing a rather large, full and security locked document case with her.'

J thought for a moment, then gave answer.

J:

'Right, get four Watchers down to the main entrance. Tell them to look out for a young woman with intent on her face, and lugging a bloody big document case in hand! Not to apprehend her, but escort her in with courtesy. Understood?'

The Plumb didn't bat an eyelid when her boss let out the swear word and assumed his autocratic manner with her. She allowed him his little ways.

The intercom fell silent. J had no concern. He knew his Plumb was fully aware of the wiles and ways of The Agency. No problem.

For his part, J sat back once more, much intrigued. Putting ETHEREAL and the Brigadier General together in one sentence, he believed useful information on the former was to hand. J did find it interesting that he hadn't heard anything, officially or on the "grapevine", as to the BG and Flowers being a business item. No matter. After all, this was The Agency, with smoke and mirrors plentiful.

And if the woman had what he thought she may possess, it would save him a lot of labour and hassle as regards to ETHEREAL. Not forgetting that Flowers herself had three Red Star security clearance. Just one below the 'Executives'.

Now, to J, it was a case of just waiting and wondering.

Enter Flowers

.... bearing manna from heaven, or as good as.

There were noises outside of J's office door, and he took it that someone had arrived. He was right; Finola Flowers, with document case in hand.

Plumb knocked on her boss's door, heard the singular word 'Enter', then opened it, steered the young lady in, closing the door behind her. No introductions. The new arrival stood before one of the most powerful men in the United Kingdom and Northern Ireland, and most certainly the undisputed Head of The Agency. It was most certainly - 'Game on'.

She seemed to stand there for an age, but in reality, just a few seconds then moved forward with intent and purpose. Finola Flowers was attired in a simple but classic matching jacket and skirt. Functional. Class, in a whisper.

The lady was about five feet six in height, well formed, figure neat, trim. There was something in her look, of the girl passing into womanhood. Hers was a quiet, muted look of beauty. Some might say she was a 'pretty girl', writers describe her as seemingly possessing an ethereal quality about her. Perhaps, but there was more substance in her look than that. Also, as J knew, she had worked for the late Brigadier General and had the three red star security classification. One didn't have those by being 'just a pretty face'. Young, barely into her twenties. Her hair was short, light brown, and she possessed bright blue eyes, themselves radiating both high intelligence and a love of life. She had straight, naturally white teeth that sat in two perfect rows, and when she flashed the briefest of smiles at J, it seemed to light up the room. Even so, the woman seemed to have an intelligence and way about her beyond her years.

Whatever, she was there for business, therefore very much in business mode.

Although J didn't know it so, in social mode, Finola could chat to anyone. She was naturally funny, exceedingly clever and knowledgeable; but never made a display of it; seemingly in second gear and sans the smart-ass approach. The BG certainly knew how to pick 'em! Finola also possessed an incredible way of reading people, and knowing how to interact with them, be they male or female. Be it at work or at leisure.

As to position, status, she didn't give a fig. To her, always the person first. She could interact with anyone; saint or sinner, God or the Devil himself. She was a peoples person, plain and simple.

As she approached J's desk, he had stood up in polite manner and simply enjoyed what approached him. He was also not slow to note the handcuffs that connected her right wrist to the handle of the document case. As she busied herself, J sat himself once more and watched on, both slightly amused and curious.

Finola had reached the desk, and begun lifting the case upward. J thought she was about to bang the document case upon it, so made haste to move in to safeguard his laptop. He need not have worried. Finola suddenly seemed to move in slow-motion, as she slowly lowered the case deftly down upon the centre of the desktop. Also, none too pleased either by the young lady's slight mischievous smile, nor of the further cluttering that assailed him. He noted the lady, of limited height, was nonetheless well fit, both in her movement, and effortlessly lifting and placing the obviously heavy case down before him.

Then, without pause, Finola produced a key from her left pocket and proceeded to unlock the handcuff on her right wrist. She then laid the key on the table next to the document case whilst, at the same time, pulling out another key, from her right jacket pocket and proceeding to unlock the case, after which placing that key also on the desk. Finola then took a step back and made her pronouncement.

FINOLA FLOWERS (FF):

'As promised, sir, my documentation on the Ethereals business, courtesy of the late Brigadier General'.

Somewhat against the moment, Finola flashed another beautifully radiant smile, then turned it off; just like a light.

A brief silence followed, then J, pointing, invited the young lady to sit herself in the seat to her right, to J's left as, in gesture, it was a command, albeit it silent and courteous. At the same time he had lifted the document case from his desktop and placed it down to the right of his chair behind the desk, then placed both the keys in his top left hand drawer.

J:

'Sit yourself, Ms Flowers; please, and may I address you as Finola, it's far more friendly'.

Finola smiled demurely, and accepted the request happily with a brief, positive nod of her head.

It was indeed 'game on', but of a kind she had not experienced before in her young, professional life within The Agency. Even so, she was up to it and, by her own endeavours, fully briefed for the hour.

The two individuals, a lifetime of experience, position and power from each other, looked steadily at each other, like respecting combatants, all be it a mismatch. For all that, appearances and circumstances were often deceptive. And there was more to the lady; considerably more.

J broke the ice in a rather unexpected way; by giving the briefest, cursory of smiles. She reciprocated, rather reservedly so. She was wondering what the wily old fox was about. After all, this *was* The Agency!

J himself was rather concerned on another matter, which involved, for him personally; a point of honour. It was clear that the young lady had spent much time and effort assembling information concerning matters Ethereal, which he believed he had to an even greater degree, enough to make hers redundant. He had to address the situation.

J (Glancing down to the document case, then back to Finola):

'I don't want to discourage you, but this Agency had a great deal of information on the Ethereal business before I came in. Possibly more than that which you've managed to put together'.

It was then that the lady made a comment that changed things , but more in the way it could enable J to present to the Prime Minister and the United States President.

FF:

'Well, sir, when the late Brigadier General asked me to research 'ETHEREAL', and I could not have done so without his considerable input, he said he would provide information, along with others he had asked to assist me as and when. As you'll see for yourself, what was provided was beyond anything I could have researched and discovered myself, let alone obtain such documentation.

He'd also suggested that when I eventually wrote up my findings, that it might be a good idea to write it in narrative form, not unlike a story, but without frills or speculation'.

BG's suggestion as to how Finola might best present any written findings was typical of the man. He'd always thought upon how those destined to read any such report from him might react, not to mention the intelligence and possible imagination of the individual recipients, and that such an approach suggested to Finola might better serve the need, be easier and more direct to the reader. J was in agreement.

Finola then added something he didn't expect at all.

FF:

When I'd suggested to the BG that I might not be best qualified to the task, he answered so: 'Softly at your side Finola, unseen we tread'.

That was it. She did not expand upon the revelation, and J thought it best not to pursue it, as for him it did not have immediate bearing on matters. As said of the man, limited imagination, and most applied to solely the task to hand at the hour.

He also justified his silence, by telling himself he was simply giving the young lady room to speak further if she so wished. For his part he knew he was neither Psychiatrist nor interpreter of dreams. Besides which, he wished to give her time and space to continue on if she wished. She did and did. He was proved justified, to a degree, as in a firm, matter-of-fact manner, Finola concluded the point.

FF:

'I found it most comforting, sir. Though not fully understanding of it, I felt both safe and able to fulfil the task'.

'Oh, how eloquently and sweet doth fair maidens lie', J thought to himself, in a none too general, silent riposte.

Finola's closing words were firm and final, and J tended to agree with her. Also, he realised that she had given him a very specific route that he could use, and which would save him both time and effort; the one he couldn't readily spare, the other he was not so inclined to expend.

J didn't waste any time in making his suggestion.

J:

'You speak well, Finola. In passing, being who and where you are, you are watched over. No harm will befall you, I assure you. In that regard, the BG was right, no matter what words he may have used'.

In truth, concerning what you have presented to me, to The Agency, although I believe all the information we have on the Ethereals would itself be sufficient unto the purpose. I also believe your input can prove most useful. Hence, I shall look at your material and, if you don't mind, lift anything that would benefit our efforts further.

I also believe that in the narrative form you've stated, it could prove invaluable, and with your assistance, I would intend to prepare it for particular and major presentation, to our Prime Minister, his senior people, and to a chosen few beyond these shores, including the President of the United States. And, just for the record, you will receive full recognition for your part in what is presented.

I'm also elevating you into the Executives, as Head of Ethereal Affairs. In this matter, you will be at my side, pretty much as an equal. Are you equal to it?'

For the first time, in look alone, Finola's surprise was evident, the news truly music to her ears. Although not overly ambitious, she wasn't adverse to advancement in her chosen profession.

Whilst she was still digesting J's words, he was forward thinking as usual. He stood up from his seat, moved around from his desk and faced Finola most directly. Even as he did so, Finola was deciding whether to chance her arm or not; to make mention of her theory concerning what she referred to as 'TEA'. She didn't get a chance, as J came in again.

J:

'Well, young lady?'

Finola herself was even surprised as to her rather honest answer.

FF:

'There are those who would think not, sir. That I'm too young, know little, should know my place, although the BG had thought otherwise.'

Although he did not express it in look, J was somewhat moved by the young ladies response. Maybe he'd read her incorrectly. To her, he left no doubts.

J:

'If you know enough, Finola, you're old enough. And on this subject, you most likely know more than I, and those who decry you, put together. Do these people who seek to belittle you, make you feel less than you know yourself to be?'

For just a moment, Finola felt even J might be doubting his decision, then her own self-belief kicked in. Jaw set firm, in defiant mood, she gave answer.

FF:

'No, sir! At least as far as this Ethereal business is concerned. I know as much as some, and a great deal more than most'.

J smiled as he responded.

J:

'That's what I wanted to hear. Leave the others to me, they'll get more than a flea in their ear, more like a boot up their collective arse, if you'll forgive my French!'

At first, Finola seemed to react in shock, then burst out with a sound of glee and displayed her most dazzling smile. She also believed J to be rather more than he seemed, a little more relaxed. Perhaps just a little more like the late BG than some gave him credit for.

J reached for his intercom, addressing Finola as he did so.

J:

'I want you to meet my right-hand woman, the redoubtable Ms Plumb. If I don't manage it, she'll scare the brownie stuff out of the backsides of any who would attempt to demean you, or attempt to 'put you in your place'. No sooner had he made the declaration, than the Plumb answered his call.

PLUMB:

'Sir?'

J:

'Miss Plumb, would you step in here for a moment, please. I want you to meet the latest addition to the Executives'.

PLUMB:

'Yes, sir'.

With that, she terminated the call her end, failing to make any comment of note. A few moments later, she entered J's room, who for his part moved over to Finola, signaling for her to stand up, then standing at her side, just as the Plumb had entered the room.

And there they were; the three together. J invited the ladies to shake hands as he explained things to his Plumb.

J:

'Ms Flowers, Plumb, knows as much as anything about these bloody Ethereals. She's going to help me put a presentation together; put it to a shape and order.

Within this office and reception, Plumb of mine, I'd like you be a Watcher to Finola. Deal with any who might express less than confidence towards her.'

As soon as J had spoken, the Plumb seemed to become as someone else again. Once more she took a rather unsure Finola's hand and shook it warmly, gently, whilst giving a lovely, almost maternal smile. When she spoke, in was in a certain resolute manner, and her words gave the recipient a different sort of confidence – and a sense of safety. Later, much later, in an unguarded moment Plumb, did confide to a colleague that sometimes she had a disquiet about Finola. That the young woman had an almost unnatural way about her: an aura. Plumb did not speak of it again, to anyone. Not even to J.

PLUMB:

'Welcome, Finola, if I may address you so. And have no fear. We young ladies must stick together; sisters against the world'.

Finola gave a soft, embracing smile, feeling almost overwhelmed. She had the feeling that there was more to the middle-aged woman than most might think. There was as she too, in her day, had an agent been.

J came in again.

J:

'Right, Ms Plumb. Take her to HR, they'll give her a new, updated ID card. Leave the old card with them. Then take her to see the Induction unit and the rest of our little kingdom. Explain the ropes as you go. Bring her back in an hour or so. Start with HR, of course, then return to them before you begin your way back, pick up Finola's new ID card; they know it's a rush job.

J then shook Finola's hand as he looked her directly in the eye.

J:

'I now you leave you to my magnificent Plumb's care, whilst I read your report. When you return to me, I want you to give me some answers re the Ethereals, off the top of your head, sans notes. Ah, yes, before you go, sign this'.

J took a blank sheet of paper from his folder and pushed it towards Finola. Without questioning, she signed, and as she did so, J caught his breath in silent surprise and excitement, but did not betray his emotions in any way. As she'd bent forward to sign the paper with her right hand, she rested her left hand on the desktop to support herself. It was there to see, as plain as a pike staff, in plain sight.

The two fingers to left and right of the middle finger, the index and ring finger respectively, of the lady's left hand were of the same length as the middle finger. And how did J know the significance? How indeed.

Once Finola had put her signature to the paper, she handed the pen back to J as she stood up straight and stepped back, smiling as she did so. Without show, J put his signature directly underneath. He then handed the paper to Plumb, instructing her to take it up to the Head of HR pronto, that they'd know what to do, as she took Finola on a grand tour. That she should pick it up on the way back. After that, for FF, it would be Ethereal, Ethereal, Ethereal.

The ladies departed, leaving J to ponder on what he'd seen.

Once alone, J thought on the young but very bright Finola Flowers. No problem, but as an old campaigner, he remembered the old adage: 'Keep your friends close, but your enemies closer'. And what might Flowers turn out to be, she with the sign of the Ethereal upon her; friend or foe?

Also, if he was right, she might possibly have another sign upon her, and not on view to sight. A small, circular, faintly blue mark at the base of her spine. Not unlike a birthmark, or a manufacturer's trademark; or who knows, even a stop-start button! He'd know when the lady underwent her compulsory medical.

J then turned his attention to the document case, and in particular, the Flowers report. When he'd finished, to him two further items gave him gist to the mill for his suspicions. For him, she could be a formidable opponent, if not a true enemy. And he? In truth, he was not so definite in answer. It took one to know one. With Ethereals, nothing was a simple affair. Friend one minute, enemy the next. And Ethereal in the singular? Neither. As had been said by one of their kind; they 'simply were'. Strangely enough, he was inclined to believe Finola would be a surrogate to the Ethereals of the Light.

And those two items? Only an insider would know their purpose: The identifying of anyone who had been recipient, victim or otherwise, of a TEAbagging (T'b for short).

So, of the two, suggested by Flowers, and how could she truly *know*, unless she'd been through the process herself, so also bearing the mark of an Ethereal? And as you ask, remember another adage: 'What's good for the goose ..... .' In other words, should the questions J (and you) apply to the woman, be put also to the man, with equal vigour.

So, exactly what were, are the two items highlighted by Flowers in her report? Herewith, the details.

'Teabagging' (T'b in abridged form)

The **T**ransferring of **E**thereal **A**bilities to another. In this case, to individuals of Humankind. Amongst other things, Flowers cited cases such as Agent 0013, Joseph Blogges. Think of what he did. Was that not just extraordinary, but simply 'out of this world'. Think also of the agent Nobel, although Flowers admits it was not a clear-cut case. Again, think of what he was able to and DID do. And then there was the Downing Street siege.

Identifying of those who had been T'b

Why would Flowers even have approached this particular concern? After all, would she not be putting the noose around her own neck? And who better to know than J? "What's it all about, Finola?" thought J, misquoting a famous film line past.

Mind you, she had a way out. She'd referred back to the point of origin, citing the JINN, who'd got her technical people to come up with a solution. They had, the red filter over camera lenses. That's how they first witnessed, first hand, the Ethereal "magic", with 'poor old' Joseph Blogges. Now, of course, J had seen further proof: Flowers and her fingers! And most likely, that other 'mark of the Ethereal'. All was madness. Madness of the so-called Ethereals. The very term meaning, amongst other things, 'unearthly' and 'celestial'.

J had questions of his own, which he did not feel obliged to disclose to others. He felt he was on the outside looking in. In reality, on the inside, wishing he was on the outside, perhaps?

Why was he unable to remember his own experience? If he himself had been T'b?

How would one know if he – or she – were a surrogate of the Light or the Dark?

Perhaps all was not as bad as it seemed, the questions not beyond answer. After all, as Flowers did point out, the Light side did rescue Humankind at the siege of Downing Street, although she didn't state it so strongly. Perhaps still giving God the benefit of the doubt, as the PM of the hour had done to the BG.

La Ronde Ethereal

Time had passed too quickly for J. Even so, he had grasped the essentials of the Flowers report, not to mention the fact it still 'did his head in', to quote a good old, down-to-earth Cockney phrase. Oh, for the simple life!

The much put upon J made use of his small, adjoining bathroom. He bathed his face, then stared hard into the mirror above the washbasin and beheld the image that faced him.

Was it all fragmenting before his very eyes? Was he quite simply himself insane – a schizophrenic?

As he dried his face, he was also aware that he was wiping away tears of frustration, anger and despair as, in disbelief, he beheld another reality of his situation.

No one had seen it thus far, J included. In truth, there was nothing there to actually *see*, unlike Finola's fingers of her left hand. Not to mention the fact that J had felt nothing, was totally unaware of his personal anatomical loss! The lobes of his ears: they were absent. Was this his own Ethereal mark? Please God, J pleaded in thought, that he was of the Light side. Himself, that is, not God, as He *was* truly THE Light supreme.

And then came the knocking at his door. J called out for whoever it was to wait. He composed himself, and then went forward to answer the call. As he did so, wondering if it was his own, beautiful nemesis. If so, then she was bloody well going down with him!

As the man strode purposely towards his door, he suddenly felt all stress and anguish drain from his person, and a lightness of being take its place.

As he opened the door gently, with an ease, a beautiful young woman stood alone before him, radiating the smile of an angel, and heaven sent. J stood back to allow her to enter. It was not his nemesis that stood before him, but a very special champion that was there to stand at his side. One an Ethereal of the Light had dispatched. The young lady entered, seemingly radiating an aura of light all around her. A trick of the light, perhaps?

* * * *

In another moment of Ethereal time, J found himself seated behind his desk, hearing a knocking at his door. It was as if he were in dream. He gathered himself and bade the caller to enter. It was the redoubtable Ms Plumb. As she entered, she appeared to be asking someone else to wait outside.

In another moment, Ms Plumb was at J's desk, informing him that the young lady had arrived, and most eager to meet him.

All was wrong, out of sequence, out of place. Yet J felt fine, albeit his mind seemed somewhat bemused, unsure. He then remembered an old motto someone often used to quote to him: 'Adapt, improvise'. So, after a few seconds of silence, he proceeded to fulfil his response, playing out a sequence he believed he didn't really have a part in.

J:

'Plumb?'

The lady was now somewhat unsure herself, but answered stoically, knowing well her boss's little ways, mind games included.

PLUMB (Firmly but respectfully):

'The young lady you agreed to see, sir. Especially when she mentioned the word Ethereal to you'.

J gave an apologetic smile to his faithful, oft put upon secretary, then waved his hand in a rather imperious, tired manner.

J:

'Okay, Plumb of mine, usher her in.'

As the relieved Plumb went to do just that, for some reason he could not fathom, J looked down to the floor, to the right of his chair. There was nothing to see, save a carpet that had seen better days.

And then the Plumb ushered in the lady, as J rose to greet her.

Yet again, he could not truly grasp the way of it, as a beautiful young lady entered and smoothly moved with a grace towards him, almost seeming to float, and Plumb was no longer in the room.

By now, the young woman was at the front of J's desk, right hand open and extended, as she announced herself.

FINOLA FLOWERS (FF):

'Finola Flowers, sir. I sincerely hope you are well, fully recovered.'

J hardly heard the words, as when he took her hand, in a moment, he seemed to remember every word the young lady had spoken some time past, both in situation and circumstance. Not to mention the contents of a document he could not remember reading, yet seemed to remember the moment he tentatively shook the hand of Finola Flowers. What she then said all but floored him, yet he sensed himself rising to the height of both joy and a full and complete understanding.

FF:

'Softly at your side, unseen we tread'.

* * * *

It goes forever on, La Ronde in its way. Around and around. Light against the Dark, ad infinitum. Alone, yet not alone.